SECOND
CHANCES

SECOND CHANCES

Brenda Chapman

DUNDURN
TORONTO

Copy Editor: Allister Thompson
Design: Jennifer Scott
Printer: Webcom

Library and Archives Canada Cataloguing in Publication

Chapman, Brenda, 1955-
    Second chances / Brenda Chapman.

Issued also in electronic formats.
ISBN 978-1-4597-0204-2

    I. Title.

PS8605.H36S39 2012   C813'.6   C2011-908006-0

1   2   3   4   5   16   15   14   13   12

  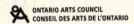

We acknowledge the support of the **Canada Council for the Arts** and the **Ontario Arts Council** for our publishing program. We also acknowledge the financial support of the **Government of Canada** through the **Canada Book Fund** and **Livres Canada Books**, and the **Government of Ontario** through the **Ontario Book Publishing Tax Credit** and the **Ontario Media Development Corporation**.

Care has been taken to trace the ownership of copyright material used in this book. The author and the publisher welcome any information enabling them to rectify any references or credits in subsequent editions.

J. Kirk Howard, President

Printed and bound in Canada.

Visit us at
Dundurn.com
Definingcanada.ca
@dundurnpress
Facebook.com/dundurnpress

Dundurn	Gazelle Book Services Limited	Dundurn
3 Church Street, Suite 500	White Cross Mills	2250 Military Road
Toronto, Ontario, Canada	High Town, Lancaster, England	Tonawanda, NY
M5E 1M2	LA1 4XS	U.S.A. 14150

*For Dawn Rayner,
my lifelong friend*

Acknowledgements

I WOULD FIRST LIKE to thank Sylvia McConnell, previous publisher of Napoleon and RendezVous Crime, for first accepting the manuscript for *Second Chances* and for all her wise guidance throughout my writing career. Thanks also to my editor Allister Thompson for his continued care and wordsmithing — I'm grateful that we are still a team. A huge thank-you to Dundurn's president and publisher Kirk Howard and to the entire Dundurn family. A special thank-you to Emma Dolan for the cover design.

Alex Brett read my manuscript early on and gave me some invaluable advice. Darlene Cole, Katherine Hobbs, and Mike Levin reviewed subsequent drafts and gave constructive criticism that made the story stronger. I am forever in all of your debt.

As always, thank you to my family and friends, new readers and old, who have supported my writing these many years. In particular, I would like to thank my husband Ted Weagle and our daughters Lisa and Julia, who are always there to cheer me on — you make it all worthwhile.

*What if they threw a war
and nobody came?*

— American slogan during the Vietnam War

Chapter One

ELIZABETH ROLLED ONTO her stomach and trailed one fingernail in a jagged line down my back. It began with the soft pressure of her fingertip between my shoulder blades, a feathery tickle on my skin that increased in pressure as it made its descent. It ended with her nail breaking through and scratching along the base of my spine above my bathing suit bottom. When Elizabeth pulled her hand away, I let out my breath and bit my lip. My back stung like crazy, but I forced myself to lie still on the blanket, letting the cool breeze from the lake wash over me. No way I'd let on she'd hurt me. I'd swallow the pain whole first.

Out of the corner of my eye, I could see Elizabeth prop her chin onto a folded arm while she stared at me through her dark sunglasses, waiting to see what I would do. Her thin lips curved into a smile.

"There oughta be a law against skin as white as yours," she said finally. "You're like a chunk of gouda cheese, for Chrissake."

"Well, it *is* the beginning of June," I said. Not that I ever tanned exactly, but I wouldn't tell her that. "You're not so brown yourself."

Elizabeth waited a few beats and said, "Compared to you, Darlene, I'm a toasted bran muffin."

She turned onto her back, then rolled off the blanket onto the sand, spreading her arms above her head and letting out a loud sigh. "I'm sooo bored. What do you do for excitement in this hick place ... or maybe I'm asking the wrong person, seeing as how you're fifteen, and lily and white could be your two middle names."

All the reasons I hated being around my Toronto cousin were coming back to me. My mother must have known how this would play out, because she'd made me promise more than once over the past week to be polite and make Elizabeth feel welcome. "Her parents are going through a hard time," my mother'd said, as if that gave Elizabeth licence to act like a turd. Like she was the only one in the universe whose parents had problems. I avoided confrontation like the plague, but I would have made an exception for Elizabeth if it wasn't for all those promises I'd made to my mother.

I knew Elizabeth was going to be trouble from the second she stepped off the Greyhound bus. She'd stood on the top of the steps, one hip thrust out while she surveyed the gas station like she was god's gift to beauty queens forced into exile in a Third World country. Then she'd tossed her long blonde hair back over one shoulder before climbing down the steps. She'd sauntered toward me across the parking lot in her skin-tight bell bottom jeans, her platform heels click-clicking on the pavement in time to the snappy movement of her hips.

"Hey, Darlene," she said when she finally reached the front door to Bill's Esso where I stood leaning against a barrel of flaming pink impatiens. I'd been left to watch for her while my mom whipped over to the grocery store after an hour of waiting for the bus to arrive. "I'd know your carrot head anywhere."

I felt a blush creeping up my neck and face. "That was my plan," I said. "Grow hair this colour so you'd recognize me."

Elizabeth laughed and flung an arm around my shoulders, squeezing a little too hard. "Still the same little cousin I remember. Easy to embarrass. It's been what, two years? You've gotten a lot taller but you're still a beanpole. Don't worry. Your chest should start coming in soon. Sixteen is the turning year."

Four insults already and we were still on hello. "Nineteen sixty-eight," I said. "Spring, three years ago. You and your parents came for the weekend."

"What makes you so sure it was then?"

"'Cause you took me to see the *Planet of the Apes* at the Elgin Theatre. It was a Saturday night." I'd also checked my diary the night before but wouldn't tell her that. Let her think I was a walking calendar. Let her think I had an elephant memory. I should have known Elizabeth wouldn't be impressed.

"Man, you have no life if that's something you remember. It's a good thing I'm here to liven up your summer."

Yeah, how lucky am I? I kept my mouth shut and followed her over to the bus driver, who was tossing luggage onto the pavement from the belly of the bus. He turned his head and smiled at Elizabeth, but she pretended not to notice. Part of leading men on was ignoring them when they showed interest. Elizabeth told me later it was dating rule number one.

I wondered if my skin had begun to burn yet. The sun was beating down on us and making the air above the sand wavy. Elizabeth moved closer and lifted her hand again to start tracing another line down my back. I jumped up like a jack in the box and pretended to wipe sand off my stomach.

Elizabeth sat up, laughing. When she finally stopped, she wiped fake tears from her eyes and said, "You should have seen your face. It was priceless."

I glared down at her but tried to sound like she hadn't pulled one over on me. "I'm going to help Mom in the store. You staying here or what?"

"I want to tan some more. I have a book to read in my bag so I won't even notice you're gone. You can run along." She raised her hand in a peace sign before lying back down.

What I'd have given to dig my foot in the sand and kick it all over her stomach. I got a few feet away and turned back. "Why'd you come to Cedar Lake anyhow?"

Elizabeth propped herself up on her elbows and scowled. "My parents made me, why else?"

"Why'd they make you?"

"Because I'm dating someone they can't stand, among other things."

"So? They can't stop you from dating who you want. These are the seventies."

"But they *can* cut off my money. Plus I flunked grade thirteen, so they're a little hard to get along with. They need time to digest that they haven't spawned a genius."

"What don't they like about your boyfriend?"

"Well, let's see. Michael's twenty-six and I'm seventeen. He plays guitar in a band, and oh yeah, he's black."

"Wow." I was impressed in spite of myself. "Your dad must have been ready to kill him ... or you."

Elizabeth smiled. "Michael came for supper once and said never again. He'd rather eat nails dipped in rat poison."

"Will you still date him when you go back to Toronto?"

She shrugged. "I was getting tired of him always asking me where I was and expecting me to follow him around, but I liked hanging out with his band. They always have good weed."

I waited a bit to see if Elizabeth would tell me anything more, but she'd stopped talking. She reached into her bag and pulled out a bottle of baby oil and a thin book that she opened half-way through.

"Well, see you later," I said.

She didn't answer. I turned around and started walking away from her. I was more than happy to put distance between us. When I got closer to the road, I started running. "Stupid cousin," I muttered. "Why couldn't you have stayed in stupid Toronto where you belong? Why'd you have to come here and ruin *my* stupid summer?"

After supper, Elizabeth plunked herself down beside me on the front steps of my mother's shop. Mom ran a convenience store in a summer cottage community on Cedar Lake in the Northumberland Hills while my father stayed in our home in Ottawa during the week and commuted to the cottage for the weekends. Mom and I had only arrived Tuesday to open up the store and we'd worked non-stop for three days setting up. Today was the first day I'd been outside, but only to entertain Elizabeth. She was the prize I got for working hard. *Some prize.* The sun had dropped a bit so that blinding sunshine struck us full in our faces. It would be a few more hours before darkness and already the mosquitoes and black flies were gathering in strength for their evening feed.

Elizabeth had on blue shorts and a gauzy white peasant top with puffy sleeves. She sucked on a grape popsicle, picking at a bug bite on the underside of her arm as she talked. Her tongue flashed dark purple every time she opened her mouth.

"I need to make some money this summer. I want to buy a stereo. I'm sick of the crappy radio."

"Just ask your parents. They have lots of money."

"They've tightened up my finances since I started hanging with Michael. Plus, there was the time they caught me smoking dope in the garden shed."

"Did they ground you?"

"They did at first, but I cried and Mom always caves. My father isn't as easy to get around and he cut my allowance. He can be a real prick." Elizabeth looked at me from under lowered lids. "So, little cousin, any ideas on how to get money?"

"There aren't many jobs around here. I babysit for a few families. Mom pays me to work in the store sometimes. Last year, I picked berries and sold them beside the highway."

Elizabeth straightened up next to me. Her mouth curved up in a mocking, sideways smile. "Man, I forget how young you are sometimes. Babysitting's what you do if you have no life. Still, it's better than nothing or *berry picking.* Easy work if the kids are sleeping. When my exile at Cedar Pond ends, I'm going to get a weekend job in a coffeehouse."

I smoothed down my smock top that had billowed in the breeze. My father would lock me in the cellar before he'd allow me to serve coffee to hippies. "Will your parents let you work while you're in school?" I asked.

"Why not? They don't have much say in what I do, or they won't once I turn eighteen. My grandmother left me some money in trust, and before you get all excited, it was on my father's side." She cupped a hand over her eyes and stared up the road, having heard the rumble of a distant engine before I had. "Do you know who's coming?"

I brushed a few mosquitoes away from my face and followed the direction of Elizabeth's gaze. A plume of dust rose like flour behind a green Volkswagen van that was barrelling up the road, fast even for the locals. Through the layer of dirt and mud smeared across the side, I could make out foot-wide purple, yellow, and red flowers painted on the doors.

"Never seen them before," I said.

We watched the van slow quickly across the road. The heads of everyone inside flopped back and forth with the suddenness of the braking.

"Drives like an idiot," Elizabeth said.

"That's funny. My father isn't due at the lake yet." I felt bad as soon as I said it.

Elizabeth made a choking sound and began laughing. "Good one."

Doors slammed. I lifted my eyes. The family was walking towards us. A man with short, curly black hair wearing a purple madras shirt and patched jeans, a woman with blonde braids and a long swoop of bangs holding hands with a boy about two years old. The boy had dark hair that hung to his shoulders in tangled curls. He was barefoot and shirtless, dressed only in red shorts. We watched their plodding journey across the street. They stopped twice and the man pointed both times to the van, but the woman just shrugged and kept walking a few steps behind him.

Good thing my father wasn't there to pass judgment. He would have shown what he thought by spitting into the dirt. The man nodded as he passed us sitting on the steps. His eyes were as black as onyx. He was good-looking. That kind of good-looking that makes your throat tighten up and your heart beat faster. When he got closer, I saw that he was older than he looked at a distance, maybe early thirties. His shirt had threads sewn into the fabric that caught the light like spun gold.

The woman stopped in front of us after the man had gone into the store. "Do you know where we could find the Davidson cottage?" Her words were a soft drawl. An image of fried chicken and grits popped into my head.

Elizabeth studied the woman's embroidered peasant blouse before her eyes rose to the silver peace sign hanging between the woman's big breasts. She wasn't wearing a bra. Elizabeth's head slowly rotated in my direction.

I looked up the road and pointed. "It's on the lakeshore road about a mile that way."

The woman leaned toward me, and I tilted my neck back to stare up at her. She had a trace of talc above her collarbone and smelled of Baby Soft perfume. Her eyes were the colour of the blue morning glories my mother planted each summer along the back fence. I could see all the way down her shirt and the sight of her large swaying breasts and dark nipples startled me.

"You are such pretty girls, sitting here in the sunshine. This your daddy's store?"

"My mother's. I'm Darlene Findley and this is my cousin, Elizabeth Hopp." I raised a finger and pointed, poking Elizabeth on the arm.

The woman pulled the little boy close until he was wrapped around her leg. The silver bracelets on her arm jangled with the movement. "This here's Sean Lewis and I'm Candice Parsens, but people call me Candy for short. Pleased to meet you girls."

Candy — like a stripper. I'd never seen one before, but figured Candy probably could pass for one. She smelled of drugstore perfume and moved as if she had no clothes on.

"Are you here for the summer?" I asked.

She nodded, "We've rented the Davidson cottage until September. I'm *so* looking forward to this summer away from the city."

The kid had begun yanking on the hem of her shirt with one hand and pounding on her leg with the other. He rubbed his sticky red mouth into her leg. Candy grabbed his fist. "Sean here has a taste for something sweet like that popsicle you're eating, Elizabeth." She looked down at him. "No hitting, Seany. I told you that. There's too much violence in this world." She smiled at us. "Darlene and Elizabeth here have the right idea, sitting on the steps and enjoying the night air. I have half a mind to join you myself."

Seany screamed up at her, a high-pitched wail that made Elizabeth and me jump. We stared at Candy to see what she'd do next. She laughed and started moving past us, holding onto Sean by one hand while he took one final swing at her thigh with the other.

"We'll see you all later then. Peace, girls," she said.

"See you later," we echoed. Elizabeth made a waist-high peace sign.

Sean's face had gone plum red and he was still screeching a little bit, angry gurgles that kept getting louder. Candy had to haul him up the stairs, his feet banging against each step. The screen door snapped shut behind them and his shrieks faded away.

Elizabeth turned to me. Her grey eyes had lightened a shade. "They seem interesting. You should really enjoy babysitting that kid."

"He looks wild. I'd rather work in the store … or shoot myself in the foot."

"I don't think he'd be so bad. Besides, aren't you curious about where they come from?"

"I'd guess from somewhere in Georgia or Texas maybe."

Elizabeth looked back up the road. "I'd like to go to the Southern States. When I finish high school, I'm going to hitchhike all over Canada and the U.S. Maybe I'll live on a commune in California and grow my own food."

"My dad will never let me go travelling around the world. He's dreaming of the day I start working full-time and bring in some money. He puts communes right up there with love-ins and Communist plots."

"Uncle George is such a Neanderthal. If he was my dad, I'd have run away by now."

"He's not that bad," I said, but I was thinking *he's way worse than bad, but I'll never tell you.*

Elizabeth wasn't listening. She'd turned on her blue pocket radio and had started singing along to Santana's "Black Magic Woman."

I pushed myself off the steps and started down the path toward the river. I grabbed a stick from the path and began beating the tall grass with one end as I walked. *Thwack. Thwack.* It felt good to hit something that wouldn't hit me back.

My life was complete torment. I wasn't allowed to do anything dangerous or exciting. My father worried every time I stepped out the door. Why couldn't I have freedom like Elizabeth? Why couldn't I live on a commune or go see the world when I turned eighteen? And more than anything, why didn't I have long blonde hair that hung straight and heavy to my waist?

I sat on my flat grey rock overlooking our little stretch of beach. I'd brought along my diary and my favourite yellow Bic fine-tipped pen. The diary was a Christmas present from Mom when I turned fourteen. Before that, I used to write in a notebook I had left over from grade six. Writing was something I needed to do, like waking up or breathing or eating Oh Henrys — I'd have to scratch words in the dirt if I didn't have paper and a pen. The cover was bubble gum pink with interlacing red hearts in the upper right-hand corner. It had a little brass key with a tarnished clasp to keep people out. I always locked my diary and kept the key hidden in my jewellery box.

My grade ten teacher had taught a lot of poetry. I liked to read it in my room on winter nights before I turned off my lamp to go to sleep. I'd written my favourite F.R. Scott line on the first page of my diary: "Ripple for a moment, the smooth surface of time". To me, the words gave voice to what I already knew. There was only a short time on Earth to do something worthwhile, but it meant breaking through the safe and the expected. I ached to do something with my life: not to look back at the end and think all I'd been was ordinary.

I'd started thinking about being a writer when I grew up. I was lousy at everything except English, plus Gideon had said the summer before that I had a knack for writing stories and essays. So far, I'd kept the writer idea to myself. Dad's big dream for me was to become a secretary when I finished grade twelve. I didn't know if I'd ever have the stomach to stand up to him. How would I tell him that I didn't want to spend my life doing something I hated that would lead nowhere — as if he wouldn't know I was talking about his life.

I wrote a few paragraphs before shutting the book. No big thoughts tonight. Even my fingers were tired.

I watched the sun sink lower into the treeline on the opposite shore. It was like looking at a painting the way the sky was layered in pinks and Creamsicle orange, and I sat there until bands of darkness rose up from the treeline and overtook the light, all the while feeling this big weight in my chest like I'd swallowed something big that was stuck halfway down and wouldn't go the rest of the way.

Elizabeth was gone from the front steps when I finally wandered up the path in the gathering darkness. There was a light on over the sign that read Findley's Store and moths fluttered around it, bumping softly against the glass. My mother would still be inside, keeping longer store hours as people trickled in for the weekend. She'd be tired but would take the time to talk to everyone and ask them how their winter had gone. I climbed the steps and pushed open the screen door. The bell tinkled, and my mother and her customers looked my way.

I didn't recognize Tyler Livingstone at first. When I did, my heart started thudding hard. I looked at him for a few seconds before I stepped closer to the magazine rack, picked up a *Mad* magazine, and pretended to read. I snuck a glance toward the counter. Tyler was paying for a couple of Cokes and bags of barbeque chips.

Jane Ratherford had one arm draped around his neck and was giggling into his ear. Jane with the long sun-bleached hair just like my cousin Elizabeth. Long, straight blonde hair — the ticket into the popular club. It didn't hurt that her father owned a Chrysler dealership in Ottawa and they lived in New Edinburgh, the subdivision bordering on Rockcliffe where all the rich stiffs lived. My family lived in Mechanicsville next to a laundromat, Freida's Suds and Soap. Freida had moved away a long time ago and left it to her son, but the name must have been too good to change. All that assonance.

I put down the magazine and looked out the front window of the shop, waiting for Jane and Tyler to leave.

"Hey, Darlene."

Crap. I turned around slowly.

"I heard you were back. Someone said your cousin's here for the summer too?" Tyler had come up behind me. His sandy-coloured hair was lightened from the sun and was longer than he used to wear it. He looked sure of himself. I might have bought his act if it hadn't been for his left eye jumping like it did when he was nervous.

"I don't get you, Darlene," he'd said last time I'd met him at Minnow Beach. "I don't get why you're mad." As if it never crossed his mind that I'd be upset when he started dating somebody else.

I cleared my throat. "Yup."

"Great. It looks like it should be a fun summer. Did you have a good year?"

"Stellar. You?"

"I made the Junior A hockey team and passed grade eleven, so I guess it was good enough."

"Coming, Tyler?" Jane asked from the doorway.

"In a sec." Tyler smiled his lopsided grin. He took a few steps away but stopped and took one back. "Your old man get much work over the winter?"

"Enough. Why?"

"I just wondered how things were going."

"Things are going great. No problem."

"Just wondered 'cause a lot of guys were laid off from the mill, like my uncle. It's been rough on his family, that's for sure."

"Dad has seniority. He'll be one of the last to go."

Tyler looked puzzled. "I thought … well, my dad must have got it wrong. Good for your family anyhow. Guess I'll see you around sometime."

"Yeah, sure," I said. I wasn't going to plan my summer around it.

I watched Tyler leave with Jane, the two of them bumping against each other and laughing as they walked toward the door. They made it hurt to breathe. I walked over to my mom and leaned against the counter. She was busy putting postcards in the wire rack standing next to the chip display. She smiled at me as her hands reached into the box of cards.

"Elizabeth went upstairs to read her book. Were you down by the lake?"

"Yeah. Just clearing my head."

"Did you talk to Tyler?"

"Not much."

"You two used to be such good friends. It's too bad you drifted apart."

"He could drift all the way to Hong Kong and I couldn't care less."

Mom looked at me and then away. "I see we have a new family at the Davidson cottage for the season."

"Elizabeth and I met them outside."

"They're a bit ... different from the usual cottagers. I was sad that the Davidsons couldn't come this year, but Mrs. Davidson wrote me a few months ago that she had a mild heart attack and they're staying in the city." Mom handed me a bag of salt and vinegar chips. "Here. You must be hungry." She kept her eyes lowered away from mine. "The man — Johnny Lewis — used to come here when we were kids. I knew his older brother but barely remember Johnny."

It was weird she was going into such detail about Johnny Lewis, because she hated gossip. I asked, "Where were they from?"

Mom paused as if she was thinking back. "New York. They owned the Bennett cottage around the point. It seems so long ago now."

Her cheeks turned a soft pink before she lowered her head, her brown arms pulling the last of the cards from the box. A lock of hair fell across her face and she didn't brush it away. Her voice was a bit odd, like it got when she was keeping something from my dad so he wouldn't get mad. I was too worked up at running into Tyler to give it much thought then. I just wanted to get away and be by myself.

"I'm heading to bed," I said.

"I'll be up soon. Just a few more things to put away." I was almost in the kitchen when she called out, "Your father will be here tomorrow. Make sure you tidy up and try not to get on his bad side."

She'd told me that so many times, it was like she said it without thinking. It worked, though. I checked the counter for crumbs and straightened the chairs on my way to the stairs by the back door.

Chapter Two

I OPENED MY EYES just wide enough to squint. Elizabeth was propped up against her headboard, reading by the sunlight that streamed in through the bedroom window. It was the same book she'd been reading at the beach, but now I could make out the title on the cover: *Love Story*.

"Have you seen the movie?" I asked as I sat up.

"Only five times. I'm going to marry Ryan O'Neal, or live with him anyway. Maybe we'll have a loft with a king-size waterbed in Greenwich Village. We'll live in glorious sin."

"That should help him get over his dead wife," I said. I'd seen the movie once and thought it sappy. I guessed I was in the minority. "You can start your own love story."

Elizabeth ignored me. "I keep hoping Ali McGraw is going to pull through but she never does. It's so sad, but that's what makes it good." Her bottom lip actually trembled. My cousin could put on an act; there was no doubt about that.

"Sad is overrated," I said.

I pushed back the covers and climbed out of bed, stretching my arms toward the ceiling. Saturday morning at Cedar Lake. My head hurt thinking about my father's pending arrival. At least the weather was going to be good. I searched through my drawers for my favourite cut-off blue jeans and a black T-shirt, then brushed my hair and let it wave around my face, knowing the more I tried to straightened it, the wilder it would go. My freckles weren't even worth bothering about. Covering them with foundation just made me look like a clown. I turned from the mirror. Elizabeth was watching me from where she rested her back against the headboard. Her staring was making me uncomfortable.

"You getting up or what?" I asked.

"I just want to finish this. I'll catch you later."

Not if I keep moving you won't. "Sure, no rush."

Mom had left a package of lemon Danishes on the counter and I grabbed one along with a glass of milk as I made my way to the store. I could hear Mom talking to somebody toward the front of the shop. I finished eating and went to see her, licking my fingers as I walked, hoping the calories would go straight to my chest.

Dad turned when I walked in, nodding once in my direction. He was still wearing his work clothes and boots and held a ball cap in his hands. His hollow cheeks worked in and out as he chewed on a toothpick. He was the reason I had my hateful red hair. His had darkened over the years into a duller auburn colour, and if there was a god, mine would too. Luckily, that was all we had in common, because he was short and broad-shouldered with pale blue eyes that couldn't hold a smile. Sometimes I pretended we weren't related and might have convinced myself it if it wasn't for the hair.

"You slept late," he said. He was straightening the gum display on the counter, aligning the packages so none was out of place. He'd be moving onto straightening the aisle of chips next.

I took a few steps closer. The smell of pulp from the mill hit my nose — a stench that his clothes held onto no matter how often my mom washed them. I imagined his skin was covered in a film of chemicals, toxic particles that sweated out of him in a thin vapour.

"Do you need me today, Mom?" I asked.

"You can go meet up with your friends. I'm okay here. I was just telling your father how much help you were the last few days."

I squinted as the sunlight caught her face. It made her brown hair golden. She was smiling at me and motioning toward the door with her eyes.

"Okay. Thanks."

I reached the magazine rack and stopped when my father asked, "Where's your cousin Elizabeth?"

"Reading in our room." I waited a few seconds, but he didn't have a follow-up question. I pushed open the screen door.

"I hope we haven't got another lazy one," I heard my father say as I started down the steps. He didn't care whether I heard him or not and that hurt more than his words. I couldn't hear my mother's reply.

I started running down the path toward the lake, trying to outrun the toxic cloud that was my father. I'd try to shake off the sick feeling I got when he was around, but it would linger like the smell of his clothes in my nostrils. I knew there was no escaping my father once he seeped under my skin.

I felt better as soon as I saw the waves rolling in ribbons onto the shore. The water was still too cold for swimming, but I took off my sandals and waded along the shoreline around the point where the community beach nestled in the bay. The frigid water felt good, like penance for my uncharitable thoughts.

Most of the cottages along the lake had their own private beaches, but everyone under the age of twenty liked to gather at Minnow Beach. I was hoping my summer friends would appear before long, and I was in luck. Danny Saunders and Michelle Cheung were sitting in the sand in our usual meeting place as if we hadn't spent a winter apart.

I dropped my sandals onto the sand and plopped down beside Danny. "Great to see you guys," I said.

"Back at you," said Danny. "We were just talking about going to find you at the store."

"Did you have a good winter?" Michelle asked after she stood up and hugged me.

"Not bad," I said. "Passed my year. Made the volleyball and basketball teams. Managed to stay out of jail … just." Spicing up my straight and narrow life with hints of walking on the wild side was better than letting on how many Saturday nights I stayed in watching *Hawaii Five-O* and *Gunsmoke*.

Michelle sat back down on the other side of Danny and grabbed his hand. He said, "Ours was much the same except for the volleyball and basketball part. We came by the store last night but you'd gone somewhere. I met your cousin Elizabeth. She's very pretty."

Michelle frowned at him. "You told me you hadn't noticed."

"I'm not blind."

"Did she say anything worth repeating?" I asked. They'd figure out soon enough that Elizabeth was only pretty on the outside.

"Just that she hates it here," said Michelle.

"What a surprise."

"She didn't strike me as someone into the nature scene," said Danny.

"She's not. I don't really know her, though. I've only spent a few nights at their house in Toronto. They visited us twice that I can remember. The last time, I was twelve and she was fourteen and all she wanted to do was chase boys at the mall."

"No malls here," said Danny. "What's she doing in Cedar Lake?"

"Her rich parents are freaking out because she has a black boyfriend who plays in a band. We're her punishment."

"Her parents are rich?"

"Stinking. Her dad is vice president of a little company that builds airplanes."

"Must be nice. Guess you're going to show her how the other half lives." Danny punched me lightly on the arm.

"Yeah, she's already let me know how much she enjoys my company."

"Did you see the family that moved into the Davidson cottage?" asked Michelle.

I stared at her. "Do you guys know everything that goes on around here?"

"What else is there to do?" Danny asked. "And you know how my mother is an expert on other people's business."

"The man is cu-uuute," said Michelle. "I heard his family used to come here for the summer when he was a kid. They lived in the States somewhere."

"That's what my mom said too. His name's Johnny Lewis and the woman is called Candy," I said.

"Candy? What kind of a name is that?" asked Michelle.

"A pretty sweet one," said Danny, rubbing his hands together.

I gave him a shove. "That was bad, Saunders."

"Yeah, but you've missed me, right?"

"I'm starting to rethink it."

"He grows on you," said Michelle, putting her arm around his shoulders. Danny gave her a kiss on the mouth before looking at me and grinning.

A dog barked from somewhere down the beach and I turned to see a man throw a stick in a high arc into the water. The dog leapt in after it and I watched for a while. I'd had a cocker spaniel puppy for a whole week once. The dog had liked to chew on things and the mess had driven my father wild, so he'd made me give it back.

"Do you want to drive into Campbellford for coffee?" asked Danny. "I got a car over the summer."

"I should let my mom know."

"We won't be that long."

"Okay."

We got up and started walking toward the road. Michelle linked her arms through mine and Danny's. "We're heading back to Kingston early tomorrow to start jobs at the Dairy Queen. My dad got us in with his friend who manages the one on Princess Street."

My shoulders drooped. "You aren't going to be here for the summer?"

"We'll be at our cottages most weekends," she promised. "We'll come back to the lake to relieve the boredom, never fear."

"I'll hold you to that."

The heaviness in my chest had returned. This summer was going to be even worse than I'd first imagined. Danny and Michelle weren't going to be around, Tyler was off with his new crowd, and I was going be stuck with my nasty cousin. It was also the first summer my older brother William wouldn't be at the lake. I didn't know how things could get any worse, but I was beginning to think they'd find a way.

I pushed open the store door, not feeling too good about disappearing for the whole day. The bell jangled as I stepped inside. Mom looked up and the creases I saw in her forehead and around her mouth relaxed. She jumped off her stool and skirted around the counter.

"I was starting to worry. It's not like you to go off without telling me. I need you to watch the store while I cook supper. Your father's gone upstairs to have a nap and Elizabeth is lying in the backyard hammock reading. You know how your father is if he doesn't get his supper on time."

"Sorry, Mom." I searched her face for signs of the mother who disappeared whenever my father showed up.

"I'll call you when supper is ready."

"Okay."

After she'd gone, I looked around the store and took inventory in my head so I wouldn't have to think about my life too much. Mom sold the staples that all cottagers needed and my eyes took stock — milk, butter, cheddar cheese, Velveeta in bright yellow boxes, Wonder bread, luncheon meats, toiletries, bug spray, popsicles, chips, gum, and chocolate bars. A rack of magazines and another of best sellers, usually Harlequin romances or mysteries, stood next to a display of fishing gear, pink and blue flip-flops, and straw sunhats. I looked down. The plank floors were coated in beach sand, and I guessed Mom had had a busy day. She could have used me but hadn't let on.

I waited on a steady stream of kids who came through the store in search of popsicles or soft drinks. There were a lot of familiar faces but some new families too. Renters were taking over the south end of the lake and the long-timers weren't pleased. They'd tried to pass a bylaw to restrict rentals the summer before, but it got nowhere. Cedar Lake proper had about three hundred people, but cottagers came to our store from adjoining lakes in more remote settings. The Findley Store was a fixture in cottageland.

At six thirty, I put the *Closed for an Hour* sign on the door and went to join my family in the little dining room off the kitchen. Elizabeth was already sitting at the table and Mom was pouring pink lemonade into plastic blue glasses at the counter. I picked up two full ones and brought them to the table before sliding into the seat across from Elizabeth.

"Did you finish reading *Love Story*?" I asked.

"Uh-huh. I need to find something else to read."

Mom set a plate of fried chicken on the table. "Why don't you girls go into Campbellford on Monday and pick up some books at the library? Elizabeth can drive my car."

"Thanks, Aunt Jan." Elizabeth made a face at the chicken when Mom turned her back, then put her hands around her throat and pretended to gag. She quickly dropped her hands and smiled at my father when he came into the kitchen and took his seat at the head of the table. Spidery red lines zig-zagged across the side of his face that he'd pressed into the pillow, and his hair was standing up on the same side. Without being asked, Mom took a cold beer out of the fridge and set it in front of him along with a plate of potatoes and green beans swimming in butter.

Dad lifted the beer to his mouth and took a long swallow. He let the bottle clunk on the table and said, "What have you two girls been up to all day?"

Elizabeth flicked a braid over her shoulder. "Just getting settled. I'm thinking of applying for work somewhere, even volunteer. I like to keep busy doing something worthwhile.

Good God, you're playing my father. "I've been delivering food to the poor," I said.

Dad ignored me and smiled at Elizabeth. "Good. Maybe, you can teach my daughter how to be productive."

Mom's hand landed on my shoulder for a second as she walked by. I closed my mouth on what I was about to say. She'd told me often enough that my smart mouth was the reason I got into trouble with my father. It was as if my vocal cords had a brain of their own.

"How did your school year go? Grade thirteen was it?" Dad asked.

"Fine. No problems, but I plan to take a year to do some volunteer work and decide what I really want to study in university."

My eyes shot over to Elizabeth. *Not only are you playing my father, but you're lying.* I noticed then that in a white cotton blouse with her hair braided into pigtails, she looked about twelve years old. She turned to my mother.

"Thank you so much for the great meal, Aunt Jan. Fried chicken has to be my favourite."

"Why, thank you, Elizabeth. I hope you found your bed comfortable last night. It used to be William's before he went off to university. We moved it into Darlene's room because that's the cooler side of the house."

"It's perfect, thanks. Is William coming to the lake this summer?"

"Maybe for the odd weekend, but he got a summer job in a law firm. He can sleep on the pullout couch in his old bedroom when he comes."

"As long as I'm not any trouble," Elizabeth said. She winked at me over a forkful of potatoes as if I was in on her joke.

I stared back but pretended I didn't catch on.

After I'd helped Mom with the dishes and watched a couple of hours of television on our flickering black and white in the tiny family room off the kitchen, I climbed the stairs to bed. I'd thought the day would never end. All I wanted was to be left alone.

Elizabeth came into the bedroom just after I'd turned off my bedside lamp and settled under the covers. She undressed by the moonlight streaming in through the window on her side of the room, then undid her hair elastic to let her blonde hair swing loose. Dressed in baby doll pajamas with her long thick hair shining platinum white where the moonlight touched it, Elizabeth could have been a fairy princess — and me, the ugly red-headed stepsister waiting in the shadows.

When she'd slipped into her twin bed, she called to me in a loud whisper. "Darlene! Are you awake?"

I deepened my breathing and threw in a snore. I opened my eyes a slit. Elizabeth was on her elbow leaning toward my bed, staring at me in the darkness. After a few seconds, she sighed and rolled onto her side facing away from me, moving around the mattress to get comfortable. Then, one more sigh before silence from her side of the room. I kept my breathing deep and loud until I was sure she was asleep. I lay awake awhile longer, watching the curtains rise and fall in the clammy breeze from the open window.

Chapter Three

ELIZABETH AND I made it to Campbellford Tuesday afternoon. We signed out some books from the town library and then walked over to Downey's Restaurant to order milkshakes. Elizabeth bought a pack of Players and some matches while we listened to the machine grinding up the ice cream. She lit up and blew the smoke away from the table out of the side of her mouth as she shook the match to put out the flame.

"Want one?" she asked and twisted her mouth into a sideways smile.

"I'm trying to cut back." Not that I'd ever smoked except the time Tyler stole a few from his mother's pack. I didn't like the taste but probably could have gotten used to it. "How long you had the habit?"

"Not so long," she admitted as she waved the cigarette around in a little circle. "I just like the smell and how I look holding one." She laughed. "You know, like Jane Fonda in *Klute*."

"Wasn't her character a prostitute? I can't remember if she smoked or not."

"Well, she looked classy anyhow, just like me holding a cigarette. Say, how do you stand being stuck in that claustrophobic little cottage every summer?"

She leaned back as the waitress set a milkshake in front of her, holding her cigarette in the air like a flag. Elizabeth's eyes widened and she smirked as she looked at the woman's orange, beehive hair. The lady had used so much hairspray, the strands were the texture of cotton candy. She turned toward me and slid my milkshake onto the table. I pretended not to notice Elizabeth's hand rise above her own head as she outlined a mound of hair. I waited until we were alone to answer Elizabeth's question.

"Summers here are all I know. Mom inherited the store from Grandpa Jack before I was born, and we've been coming to the lake every summer since."

"Yeah, I heard the story from my mom." Her voice got sing-songy. "Your mom got the store because Uncle George wasn't making much money, while my dad's rolling in it. Without the store, who knows what would have happened to you. Plus, everyone felt sorry for your family after what happened to Annie."

She paused again and studied me. Her eyes were like a cat's, watching and waiting for the mouse to move. The mouse was me.

I smiled and pretended that her mentioning Annie didn't bother me. "It was fun coming to the lake when I was younger, but it isn't as exciting now," I said. No way was I going to talk to her about Annie. No way.

"I couldn't imagine being stuck here with my parents," Elizabeth said. She pounded the cigarette into the ashtray and it split in half. "Well, I wouldn't have to worry about that since Daddy never leaves his office long enough to have a bloody vacation. If he and my mother ever went anywhere together, I'd know the end of the world was near."

I searched for something to steer the conversation away from my family. "What's your boyfriend like?" I asked.

"Michael? He's very hip … and cute. He sings in a band and doesn't do much else. My parents have no idea how to take him, since all they think about is making money and keeping up with the rich neighbours, and he's just the opposite. They can't stand the very idea of me dating Mick, especially since he's black. They're scared their grandkids will be a mocha-coloured embarrassment. I should get pregnant just to see their faces crack."

"A good reason to bring another kid into the world."

"Yeah, well. It would give my parents something to unite over. God knows they don't agree on anything else, with the possible exception of looking down on those less fortunate." Elizabeth lit another cigarette as she talked and blew a stream of smoke at me.

"I thought you wanted to make money," I said.

"Well, it drives my parents wild to think I'm turning up my nose at their lifestyle, so I can pretend for a while … and it keeps Mick interested." After a pause, her eyes zeroed back in on me. "Your father's gotten kind of fixated about things. Everything in its place, nobody out of line."

"He likes things done a certain way."

Elizabeth flicked the ash of her cigarette onto the table and swept it onto the floor with her fingertips. "That's the biggest understatement I've heard all week. My way or the highway, more like. Was he like that after he came out of the hospital? You know, obsessive about everything?"

I looked into Elizabeth's grey eyes and wondered how much she knew. She stared back at me without blinking. I took my time answering.

"My dad is how I've always known him. He ... worries."

"Mom says he wasn't always so angry. That he got that way after the accident."

I shrugged then looked past her out the window. *Annie.* I didn't want to get into it with Elizabeth. I didn't want to get into it with anybody.

"Did I tell you that we have William over for dinner quite often in Toronto?" she asked.

I swung my eyes back to her face. "Really? He's never mentioned it to me."

"Your brother's gotten cute. He's so serious about human rights and marching against the war. Not to mention, he's going to make lots of money when he becomes a lawyer. If he wasn't my first cousin ..." Elizabeth laughed. She tilted her head to one side, looking me over. "You don't resemble him much."

"No."

"Annie and William looked like your mom when they were little. My mom has a photo album. You look like somebody else's kid altogether."

"I dream that I am. Sometimes, I believe another set of parents will come find me and take me away from all this."

On cue, the front door to the restaurant opened, and I broke away from her gaze. *Crap encore.* Tyler Livingstone was standing in the doorway looking around. I slumped down in my seat and watched him head toward the counter. He was wearing a Boston Bruins T-shirt and cut-off shorts that were frayed at the bottom. He'd put on muscle since the summer before. The sight of him made my heart beat faster, like a little clock running a race. Elizabeth followed the direction of my eyes.

"Somebody you know?"

I snapped my eyes back to her face. "Tyler Livingstone. We used to hang out when we were younger before we outgrew the kids in the sandbox thing." I didn't want her to take an interest in Tyler … or to know of mine. Hopefully she'd never find out that Tyler and I had been inseparable until the summer before.

"Ready to go?" Elizabeth gave me a big smile and took a final suck on her straw. She reached for her macramé bag. "I'll pay for these. My treat."

She jumped out of the booth before bee-lining it over to the cash to stand next to Tyler, who was ordering some food to go from the waitress with the big orange hair. He was leaning on the counter and turned his head to look at my cousin. I got up more slowly but made it over in time to hear her say, "Hi. I'm Elizabeth Hopp. Darlene's older cousin from Toronto. She tells me you spend summers at the lake too." Elizabeth extended her hand.

Tyler pushed himself off the counter and shook it. He looked past her to me. "Oh, hi, Darlene. I didn't see you standing there. How's it going?"

"Just fine. You working this summer?"

"I start a road construction job tomorrow, but I'll be able to spend nights at the lake."

"We're spending nights there too," said Elizabeth. "It sure is getting hot, isn't it? I hope July doesn't get too unbearable."

She pulled the top of her shirt open and shut a few times like she was letting off steam. I could see the crack between her breasts when she pulled her shirt open one last time.

Tyler looked at my cousin as if he was running her words around in his head. I didn't need to give them any more thought. I knew exactly what she meant.

"There's the bill." I pointed to ours by the cash. "A dollar fifty."

"Yeah, yeah," said Elizabeth. "Where's the fire?" She pulled some money from her bag and took her time putting it on the counter. "It sure was nice meeting you, Tyler Livingstone. We'll be seeing you around then." She smiled in his direction, full wattage.

"Sure. See you around sometime," Tyler said and grinned sideways at me before leaning back on the counter to wait for his food.

Of course, he might have been directing his smile at Elizabeth, but I wouldn't let myself think about that or I'd stop breathing for good.

~••~

The next two days passed slow as syrup. My mother noticed that I was avoiding my cousin and called me into the store.

"You're not being very cousinly," she said from where she sat on her stool behind the counter. "Elizabeth has been moping around and you're nowhere to be seen."

"I'll try to be better," I said, "but she makes it hard."

"Well, you try harder," Mom said before she went back to doing her crossword puzzle. Without raising her head, she added, "She's out back."

Elizabeth looked up from where she was lying in the hammock as I crossed the lawn toward her. I plopped down on the grass nearby. From my position, I could see my mother's garden and glimpses of the lake past the pine trees at the back of our property. Bees were buzzing in the climbing rose against the house and the air was hot and still, as if someone had turned on a space heater. Elizabeth kept one foot on the ground and rocked herself slowly back and forth. Every time the hammock swung to its highest point, she'd hold herself there and stare at me before letting it swing back through the shadow of the spruce tree. Her purple-tinted granny glasses made her eyes look big and owlish. She was freaking me out, which I knew was her plan. Her little blue radio sat next to us on the lawn. Cat Stevens was singing about a hard-headed woman.

"Do you want to come with me to see Gideon?" I offered when I couldn't take being watched anymore.

"Who's Gideon?" Elizabeth's head bobbed up again.

"The guy who delivers the mail. He lives on the other side of the lake. He also writes a column for the *Globe and Mail*. Mom always talks to him when he brings our mail. Last summer I didn't have much to do, so I started going over to his place to find out about writing for a newspaper. We sort of hit it off." I didn't tell her that the reason I was bored was because Tyler had deserted me for his new friends.

"How old is he?"

"I don't know. Fifty-something."

"He's old enough to be your grandfather. You're not the prettiest girl on the block, but even you could do better than that."

"Gee, thanks."

"You have so much to learn. Fifty-year-old men don't hang around with fifteen-year-old girls for their intellect, believe me."

"Is that another Elizabeth rule of dating?"

"Yeah. Rule number two. Never date a man over twice your age. Someday they'll be pushing a walker and you'll be wishing they could just get it up one more time."

"I should take notes."

"You should. Someday my advice could be a best-seller. Like that woman in the paper."

"Dear Abby?"

"Yeah, her. I could start a column and get rich and famous."

I laughed. "The thing is you have to know what you're talking about. Gideon is *not* interested in me like that, so you're wrong about him. Have *you* ever dated an older man?"

"I went out with a phys ed teacher for a semester, but he wasn't that old."

"Couldn't he have gotten into trouble dating a student?"

Elizabeth smiled. "Of course. That was why I did it."

"Well, I'm going to see Gideon and will try to keep all your brilliant pointers about men in mind."

I pushed myself up from the ground to go find my mother and let her know where I was going. I'd tell her I'd tried hard to get Elizabeth to come with me but she didn't want to. Maybe Mom would buy it. I'd be happier visiting Gideon alone anyway, once I shook off Mom's sigh and the disappointed look that I knew were coming.

I liked the hot sun on my arms and legs as I biked to Gideon's. It felt like a thick wool blanket keeping me warm. Trickles of sweat ran down my back where the strap of the knapsack chafed across my shoulder. The road veered away from the lake for the first while and then swooped back so that I followed the sun sparkling on the water for the last half mile. I could hear the drone of flies in the bushes lining the road and now and then crows cawing from the higher tree branches.

Just when I was starting to really cook in the heat, Gideon's little pine cottage came into view. It was built on a crest of land that overlooked the bay. Gideon lived alone except for his goat Nanny, four hens, a rooster, and a black lab named Ruby. He was one of the few who stayed in his cottage over the winter, maybe because he wasn't all that happy hanging out with people. Anyone could see that if they read his opinion column in the Saturday *Globe*. I especially liked the fact that he railed against all things stupid, most of all the Vietnam War, which I thought a total waste of effort.

"I was a big gun once," he'd told me the summer before. "Not sure it made me happy. I like it better now, weeding the garden, writing poetry, and not dealing with idiots on a daily basis." He didn't look like a poet, but just goes to show.

I found Gideon in the garden staking up bean plants. He was wearing denim coveralls and a wide-brimmed straw hat, and I thought he looked older than the summer before. His face got happy when he saw me — well, happy for Gideon, which amounted to a quick smile and his hand running up and down through his beard.

"Darlene Findley. You're a sight for my sore eyes. Did you grow a foot over the winter or am I sinking?" He straightened awkwardly and started walking toward me. Ruby leapt ahead and jumped up on my legs. I bent to rub her head.

"I'm a growing machine," I said. "Just call me Twiggy with red hair."

"Twiggy started a fashion revolution, if I recall. You might be the next one if you're not careful."

"I wouldn't hold my breath. Red hair and freckles on a bean pole aren't likely to cause any riots."

"None of that now, Little Fin. Come up to the house

and I'll get you something cold to drink. You look like you've been in the sun more than is good for you."

His brown eyes saw too much when they looked at me, and I was happy to turn around and lead the way to his back door with Ruby bounding through the tall grass ahead of us.

It was cooler in his front room. A ceiling fan was moving the soupy air around, and I plunked myself directly under it on the couch. Gideon set a glass of lemonade for me on the coffee table. I looked over to where his navy blue mail bag hung on a hook by the door.

"You're still on mail duty?"

"For now. Thinking of giving it up, though. I'm busy with writing and the house. New people in the Davidson cottage this summer," he said, settling into his desk chair. He spun it around so he was facing me. "They have different last names but that could mean nothing. People get married nowadays and women keep their last names. Women's lib they call it."

"I met them. Well, I met her anyway. They have a little boy too." I hadn't thought about Candy since talking with Danny and Michelle about the new family staying in the Davidsons'.

"I delivered a package up there this morning. They were still in bed and it was close to eleven thirty. Your cousin Elizabeth Hopp got a letter this morning too. She from Toronto?"

I nodded. "She's been sent to stay with us for the summer. Her parents figure a summer with me will straighten her right out."

Gideon shook his head. "They've got to be dreaming. If she likes the fast life, a summer at Cedar Lake won't change her. She'll just come up with new ways to amuse herself."

"You don't think people can change?"

"Only if they want to … or have to. People are basically selfish, self-serving hedonists. I could go on now, but we have all summer."

I laughed and Gideon smiled again. His smiles never hung around for long, and it always felt good to be the cause of one. "How was your winter?" I asked.

"Not bad. Caught a cold, though, and am having trouble shaking the cough. Ruby developed a bit of arthritis in her hind legs."

"Poor old Ruby," I said, rubbing her back. She let me fuss over her for a bit before getting up to go lie at Gideon's feet.

"How's your writing going? Win any school essay-writing contests this year?" Gideon's eyes studied my face. I would have liked him not to be watching me so intently.

"No. I didn't enter," I said and looked down at my leg. I swiped at some dirt on my knee.

"But you won last year. What was your topic again?"

I kept my head down. "Sending more aid to starving people in Biafra."

"That's right. Why didn't you enter again with all that success?"

I thought of how Dad had torn apart my ideas after I'd won. He'd said we should be keeping our money in

Canada and helping our own people first. "I just didn't have time," I said.

Gideon kept looking at me over the rim of his glass but he didn't say anything. I set my glass on the coffee table.

"Thanks for the drink, Gideon. I guess I'll be getting home to give Mom a break from the store."

"Your lovely mother. Say hi for me. Your dad still commuting on the weekends?"

"Yup. He's fulltime in the mill since last year."

"That's good. I know it's a rough go for your folks when he's not working."

He let the implication lie between us. I didn't pick it up. Family solidarity and all that. We walked toward the door.

"I hear there's a beach party for you kids Friday night. I guess you'll be taking your cousin Elizabeth."

"Maybe."

"Next time you stop by, I should have my new poem done. I've tentatively called it 'Alcoholic Haze on the Northumberland Hills.'"

"All your poems seem to follow a certain theme, Gideon."

"Write about what you know, kid. Lesson number one."

"Between you and Elizabeth, this summer should be quite an education."

"Your cousin teaching you something?"

"You might say that. I figure I'll be well-rounded by the time she leaves, or so screwed up, I'll never get a date."

"Soak it all up, Little Fin. You never can take in too much information, no matter how extraneous it appears at the time."

"What does extraneous mean, Gideon?"

"Irrelevant. Superfluous. Unnecessary."

"Like studying math or reading *Love Story* for the tenth time?"

"The very same. Although it's beyond me why anyone would stoop to read that pulp even one time. It's like people nowadays get their taste in a box of Cracker Jacks."

I braked in front of Candy Parsens' driveway and stood with both feet on either side of bike, my back resting against the seat. I looked towards the cottage. It was set well back from the road and almost completely hidden from view by two maple trees, a stand of birch, and a tangle of shrubs that needed cutting back. From where I stood, I could hear loud music pouring out of an open window. Janis Joplin was singing "Me and Bobby McGee," and I rested for a minute to listen. The album had been released in January after she'd died, and I hadn't heard it all the way through. I looked back toward the house. What would it hurt to check out how they were doing?

I got off my bike and followed Janis's gritty voice up the drive and through the bushes to the far side of the path that wound through scrub along the front of the building. Around the corner of the cottage, I found Candy bent over a clothes basket, lifting a shirt to pin on a line she'd strung between two trees. Her white peasant skirt billowed around her legs as she reached to clip the clothes peg. Her feet were bare and I could see her breasts spilling over a red tube top. This time, her blonde hair was wound into a knot at the base of her neck, but pieces had escaped and hung down her back in uneven strands. When she looked in my direction, she cupped a hand over her eyes. It took her a few seconds to recognize me. She started walking in my direction, her smile wide.

"It's Darlene, isn't it? Darlene from the store? It's so good to see somebody familiar. I can't tell you how much."

When she was just a few feet away, she stopped. "Would you like something cold to drink? I've just squeezed some lemons. It was as if I knew I'd have company today. It's good karma."

She looked so hopeful, it didn't feel right just leaving. I nodded. "That'd be nice. Thanks."

Candy talked non-stop as we walked toward the back door. I left my bike leaned against a rain barrel and followed her dancing feet into the kitchen. When I stepped inside, it took me a second to take it all in. The counter was filled with torn bags of flour and brown sugar, containers of granola cereal, whole wheat pasta, and different beans and grains that I couldn't place. The sink overflowed with dirty dishes while half-full coffee cups and bowls of milk and cereal lay scattered across the table. I could see glass ring stains and the freshly burned outline of a pot on the counter near the stove, now caked in a layer of grease. A bag in the corner spilled over with garbage. The smell of food left too long in the sun mixed with rotting fruit and burned coffee made me breathe in shallow gulps. I figured Mrs. Davidson would have a bigger heart attack if she dropped by unexpectedly.

Candy noticed my neck swivelling back and forth to take it all in. She waved a hand at the mess and said happily, "Doesn't take us long to settle in. We can sit outside if you like. I'll just get the lemonade."

"I'll wait outside." I tried to speak without inhaling.

Candy pushed open the screen door with her hip a few minutes later and stepped outside. She handed me a glass as she sat down next to me on the back steps. I sipped the fresh lemonade, and it was good, better than Gideon's store-bought stuff. Candy took a long drink, then reached inside the pocket of her skirt and pulled out a crumpled package of cigarettes and a red Bic lighter. She lit one and inhaled deeply, letting the smoke come out of her nose like a head of steam.

"That's better. I've been washing clothes by hand all morning and needed a break."

"Where's your little boy?" I'd forgotten his name.

"Seany? He's having a nap. I've never met a kid who likes to sleep as much as this one. He's up half the night, mind you." Candy turned sideways on the step and looked at me. "You've gotten some sun today. Do you like being outside? I personally can hardly stand being indoors."

"I'm outside as much as I can be. I burn easily though."

"I guess with your colouring. You have such lovely creamy white skin. I love your freckles."

"Are you *kidding*?" I said without thinking.

"Not at all. I'll bet you hate how you look, am I right? We all want to look like some other overpaid, cookie-cutter fashion model. It's all a load of brainwashing from corporate America. You are a natural beauty. Boys'll be falling all over themselves to go out with you in a few years. Just you wait and see."

A few people had told me that I was unusual look-ing, but that hadn't felt like a compliment. I looked at her with a greater interest. The cigarette moved up and down between her lips as she talked.

"Wouldn't it be nice to go for a swim?" Her eyes were wide and sparkly. "Johnny doesn't like me to leave Sean with a sitter or even go outside when he's in his crib, but maybe one afternoon when Sean's sleeping, we could sneak to the beach for an hour. Seany's dead to the world for a few hours every day."

I'd never heard an adult speak like this before. I sat still thinking about what she'd said. "Why doesn't your husband want you to leave Sean with a sitter?"

Candy laughed as if I were the most amusing per-son on earth. "Says we've uprooted him and he wants the kid to have some stability for a while. My *husband* Johnny is a strange man."

She swept her cigarette in a wide arc to take in the property. She looked at me and her eyes were shiny with tears. "This is a far cry from my old life. Do you know I used to be a back-up singer for a couple of bands? I lived in L.A. for a while and dated rock singers. It was a great life."

"So why did you give all that up?"

"I fell for Johnny. Simple as that." Elizabeth said the words as if free will had nothing to do with it. The cigarette in her hand was trembling. "Sure, he's five years older than me, but we just had a connection, you know? Johnny just had this aura and I knew I was destined to be with him. It's our karma."

That karma word again. "Did you date or know anyone famous ... I mean, before Johnny?"

"Famous? Of course. I used to hang out with Janis Joplin — I still like to play her music in the morning to kick-start my day. It takes me back, you know? I was devastated when she died in L.A. They asked me to speak at her funeral, but I was too ripped apart to get up in front of all those people. Jesus, I miss her still. Her high school voted her the ugliest girl, did you know that? How do you get over something like that? People can be such monsters." She shook her head. "We used to zip around L.A. in her Porsche. It was painted all psychedelic colours and everyone watched us go by, like we were really something. We had such a blast when we were together. Those were the days, my friend, to quote another musician pal of mine."

"Wasn't she that Welsh ...?"

"Singer. Yes, Mary Hopkin. I met her when I was over in Britain one summer. We toured around together."

Candy was friends with Janis Joplin and Mary Hopkin? Elizabeth would kill to hear Candy's stories. She wanted to meet somebody famous even more than I did. Candy touched my bare arm with her fingers.

"Janis was troubled, you know? And the drugs … well, that's what did her in. I was supposed to be with her that night but met up with Jimmy and that was that. It hurts to think I could have saved her."

"Jimmy?"

"Jim Morrison. You ever heard of him?"

I nodded. I forced my lips back together. Everybody under the age of thirty had heard of Jim Morrison and the Doors.

Creases appeared in Candy's forehead and her eyes got worried. "You won't tell? Johnny hates when I talk about the old days and living in the States."

I shook my head.

"Speaking of Johnny, he should be back within the hour, so I'd better get Seany up and get him bathed and ready to see his daddy."

"I should be going too."

I stood and she took my empty glass from me. I'd been hoping for a few more of her stories.

Candy looked up at me with her crystal blue eyes and a crooked smile, as if she could read what was going on inside my head. "Won't you come back tomorrow? We could swim in the bay. If you feel weird about leaving Sean alone, you could watch him while I do some lengths. Johnny has an appointment in Toronto and he'll be gone early. You don't know how much that would mean to me if you could come by."

"What time?"

"Johnny's gone for the day, so one o'clock would be perfect."

"I should be able to make it then."

"And remember, not one word about us living in the States. Johnny would kill me if he knew I was talking about my past life. He just hates me talking about those days to anybody."

Chapter Four

THE NEXT MORNING, I moped around the house, listening to the rain beating against the roof. A wind from the east buffeted the cottage without signs of letting up. Nobody made the trip from their cottage to the store, and I couldn't blame them. Mom was bored and called me and Elizabeth for lunch earlier than usual. She set bowls of Campbell's tomato soup with sandwiches of ham and mustard on white Wonder bread in front of us. Elizabeth looked at the food as if it was full of bugs. Mom went back for a jug of milk. Elizabeth leaned into me and said so low only I could hear, "I wonder what the poor people are eating."

I picked up my spoon. "Mom defrosted a Sarah Lee orange cake for dessert. Save some room."

Mom slid in across from me. She rested an elbow on the table and cupped her chin in her hand. She sighed. "It's going to be an all-day rain. I guess we better get used to the idea." She sighed again and looked out the kitchen window at the rivulets of rain running down the window pane. The dark, wet day caught me deep inside and made me feel depressed. I'd given up the idea of swimming with Candy at one o'clock.

"Yum, great canned soup," Elizabeth said to my mother. "Hits the spot on a rainy day."

"Glad you like it," said Mom. "This soup is Darlene's favourite."

I took a slurp from my spoon and grinned at Elizabeth. "It goes even better with Klik sandwiches," I said.

Elizabeth grimaced. "What in the world is Klik?" she asked.

"It's that meat the colour of lung that comes in a can with a key. The best part is the jelly they preserve the meat in. All nice and gushy in your mouth."

Elizabeth's pursed her lips together like she was holding something in.

I lowered my head and smiled. "Just what do the Hopps eat for lunch?" I asked as if I cared. I set my spoon down and stared at Elizabeth. "You know, like on a regular rainy day."

Mom lifted her chin from her hand and looked at me.

Elizabeth smiled and her eyes glinted. "Cook whips up something. Quiche Lorraine or Coquilles St. Jacques. Whatever's on hand. She makes a terrific French onion soup from scratch. Croutons toasted in the oven and mozzarella cheese bubbling until it's just brown on top."

"This must be quite a change for you," I said. "How can you bear life without professional help?"

Elizabeth's smile turned into her familiar smirk. "You might benefit from some professional help yourself."

Mom cleared her throat. "Darlene," she said quietly.

I broke away from my cousin's stare and looked down into my bowl of soup. "Do you need me in the store this afternoon, Mom?" I asked, scooping up a spoonful and raising it to my lips.

Mom stared back at the rain that was rattling the glass and streaking down the window. The worry lines on her forehead deepened. "I should be fine. There won't be much business if this weather keeps up."

"What do you do when it rains?" Elizabeth asked me.

Mom turned her attention to me and offered encouragement with her eyes.

"We could play a board game or cards if you want," I offered half-heartedly. *For the love of god, say no.*

Elizabeth pulled all her hair into a knot on top of her head, then let it cascade over her shoulders before answering. "Well, I'm tired of reading, so I guess."

"Do you know how to play rummy?"

"Not that well. We could try a few hands."

"I'll clean up here," said Mom in her fake cheery voice, the one she used when things weren't going as well as she would like. "Nobody will come to the store until the rain lets up."

We climbed up to our bedroom and sat on the floor. Elizabeth tuned her radio until Joe Cocker's gravelly voice filled the silence. The reception was filled with static and she played with the knob for a bit, trying to tune it better. She hit the side of the radio with the palm of her hand a few times before setting it on the bedside table and sitting down across from me. I shuffled the deck of cards.

"Bloody storm is messing up the reception. This never happens in Toronto." Her face was one big pout.

"So we each get seven cards ...." I began.

Elizabeth interrupted, her voice bored. "I remember how to play. It's not that difficult." She reached into her pocket and pulled out the pack of cigarettes.

"So why did you say you didn't know how to play?"

"It amused me. I have to find my fun where I can get it. You make it easy."

"Mom won't like you smoking in the house."

Elizabeth shrugged and took one out of the pack. She studied it for a second before waving it a few inches in front of my face. "What she doesn't know won't hurt her." She stood and pushed the window open. It was an old casement window that took effort to budge. Rain quickly filled up the sill. She dropped back down onto the floor and sat with her legs crossed and took out her matches. "There. Happy now?"

I picked up my cards moved them into sequence. "As a clam," I said.

We played the first hand and Elizabeth slapped down a trio of aces, chortling through the smoke she blew between us. "Take that, little cousin."

"Good one," I said. I picked up the queen she'd laid down. One more and I would have a run in diamonds.

Elizabeth squinted at me through a haze of smoke. "Oh, by the way, did I forget to mention that Tyler came around yesterday while you were visiting that old guy?"

"Gideon."

"What?"

"The old guy. His name's Gideon." I discarded the two of clubs. Excitement fluttered in my stomach. *Don't let Elizabeth know.* "Did Tyler want anything?"

Elizabeth's eyes landed on me like I was a piece of something shiny. I looked back down at my cards.

"He wanted to make sure we knew about the beach party this Friday night. Did you know about it?"

I squirmed a bit under her stare. Maybe, I should have told her. "They happen most weekends during the summer. We light a campfire and somebody always brings beer. We can go together if you want."

"And do you drink beer?"

"Like a fish."

"Why do I find that hard to believe?" Elizabeth discarded the nine of hearts.

"I don't know. Why is that?" I laid the three of clubs on top of the nine.

Elizabeth leaned her head to one side and studied me. "I detect something going on under your square, placid exterior." She shuffled the cards in her hand before placing a row of fives on the floor, then discarded a queen. Her voice got friendlier. "You know I'm just kidding around, don't you, Dar?"

"Sure." I picked up the queen and pretended to think over my hand. Before Elizabeth said anything, I laid down a four-card straight, three fives, and discarded the last card in my hand. "Rummy," I said. I said the words quietly so she wouldn't think I was gloating.

Elizabeth dropped the rest of her cards onto the floor in front of her. "Damn. I only needed a king." She smiled at me. When her grey eyes lit up, she was pretty enough to be one of the models in *Seventeen* magazine. "Let's be friends, Dar," she said. "I'm sorry if I hurt your feelings. I guess I have to remember that you are so much younger than me and don't always get my teasing. We're cousins, joined by blood, and that makes us joined for life."

"Yeah, I guess." I couldn't tell whether she was still playing me or being serious. It didn't really matter. I collected the cards and handed them to her. "Your turn to deal," I said.

I found Mom in the store leaning on the counter reading the June edition of *Better Homes and Gardens*. She glanced up at me and smiled as I slipped in beside her and pushed myself up onto the stool. "How's it going?" she asked.

"Okay. Elizabeth is having a nap."

Mom bumped her leg against mine. "Thanks for playing cards. How was Gideon the other day?"

"Okay, except he has a cold. After I biked to his place, I stopped by and saw Candy. We had lemonade on her back steps."

Mom frowned. "Oh? I'm not sure that's a good place for you to be hanging around."

"Candy just seems lonely. Johnny isn't there much."

"They have nothing in common with you, Darlene. I'd really rather you didn't start going over there."

I was puzzled. My mother usually was accepting of everybody. "I won't," I said, but only so she wouldn't worry. No point telling her about the swimming date.

Mom turned and looked out the window. "We could do with more customers, but the storm is getting worse. I have a bit of a headache."

"Why don't you go lie down? I can watch the store."

"You must have something better to do."

"I'll just read one of the books in the rack and maybe sneak a chocolate bar."

"Sneak two if you want."

Mom closed up the magazine and patted me on the shoulder before she walked out from behind the counter. She fussed with straightening up the gum display and I knew she wanted to tell me something. Finally, she looked up. "How are you and Elizabeth really getting along?"

"Okay, I guess."

"You don't mind sharing your room?"

"I'll survive. She's keeping my summer interesting."

"I'm not so sure this was the best place for her to spend her holidays. Your aunt Peg just had so much to deal with." Mom bit her lip. "Oh, by the way, William phoned and said he'll be home next weekend for a few days."

I clapped my hands. "I can't wait to see him. Will Dad be here tomorrow?"

"Uh-huh. As far as I know. He should arrive by suppertime. We'll have to think of something good to feed him. Maybe I'll take a run into town tomorrow morning and pick up a few things. A pork roast might be nice. Your father likes that. Do you think you could get up and watch the store for an hour or so?"

I looked hard at my mom. The rosy colour had crept back into her cheeks again and her eyes were fixed on something to the right of my head. I was surprised because she normally had Dad bring in supplies Friday on his way to the lake.

"Okay," I said at last.

Mom nodded and turned up the radio. The Guess Who was singing "These Eyes."

"I love this song," Mom said, jumping off the stool. She pretended to waltz with someone across the floor on her way to the kitchen, twirling and spinning between the rows of canned food. She looked pretty in her white shorts and sleeveless blouse patterned in tiny violets and brown sandals showing off her long legs. I wondered if she minded being away from Dad all week. I'd never thought about it before. I'd never much considered whether my mother was happy with her life — she was just my mom. It was as if a door had opened in my mind, and I wasn't sure I wanted to go through it to find what was on the other side.

Mom stopped at the back of the store and threw me a kiss. I smiled and threw one back. And then, she was gone.

I woke up earlier than Elizabeth. The storm had moved on and full sun beamed onto the floor through the gap in the curtains. It was Friday — the day my dad was coming, the day of the beach party. I lay in bed a while longer, drifting in and out of sleep, dreaming Tyler Livingstone had asked me to walk with him on the beach. We were sitting side by side in the sand then suddenly we were ten years old and he was pushing me on the tire swing my dad had hung from the branch of the old oak tree at the back of our property. Tyler was calling up to me, but I couldn't hear what he was saying. My feet touched the leaves on the branches every time he pushed me higher, and I felt like I was flying. I looked down from my place in the sky and Elizabeth had appeared. She had her arms around Tyler's neck and was kissing him on the mouth. I yelled to Tyler to get me out of the tire, but he didn't stop kissing Elizabeth, and I couldn't get down. I struggled to free my legs while Elizabeth and Tyler spun around and around on the grass beneath me, Elizabeth's arms spread wide and her face turned up to the sky, a smirk on her face the size of a half moon.

I jolted awake. I was lying on my stomach, my face pressed into the pillow and the bed sheet tangled around my sweaty legs like a cloth bandage. I kicked away the sheet and rolled onto my back, then swung my feet onto the floor to sit on the side of my bed. Across the room, Elizabeth was still sleeping, her back to me and her long blonde hair messy in sleep and trailing across the pillow like ropes of seaweed. I didn't need to talk to her yet, the only good thing about waking up so early.

I padded to the dresser and grabbed some shorts and a T-shirt to change in the bathroom. I felt for my diary where I'd stashed it under my bed and collected the key from my jewellery box. Elizabeth's breathing was deep and even. I walked quietly out of the room, got dressed, and went downstairs.

Mom wasn't up yet, even though bright sunshine streamed in through the windows. I stopped near the kitchen window and craned my head to look past the tree branches to the cloudless sky. The outdoors was calling to me. I'd find somewhere quiet to write before Mom woke up and wanted me to look after the store. I'd have time to rid myself of Elizabeth and Tyler and the disturbing vision of the two of them that I'd conjured up.

The path felt like my own private entrance through the pines and cedars to the sheltered bit of beach where I'd spent hours swimming and sitting on the rocks or the sand, watching the waves roll across the shoreline. It was my special place this early in the morning, before other cottagers made their way to the public beach just around the bend from our tiny stretch. Gulls circled overhead and their shrieks were startling within the morning's silence. A slight wind across the lake was kicking up waves that rolled one after the other onto the shoreline. I shivered inside the sweater that I'd put on before leaving the cottage, but it wouldn't be long before the sun started warming up the air and the day turned hot.

The rocks were wet and slick, so I placed my feet carefully. I climbed slowly upwards until I reached my favourite flat rock looking out over the lake. It was still cool and damp on the rock where the sun hadn't had time to bake away the night's chill. I didn't mind the cold on my legs and sat so that my back was against a boulder and my feet were dangling over the edge. I took a minute to watch a gull searching the sand for something to eat before I opened my book and started writing.

The words came easily. I wrote about my dream. I recorded the slights inflicted on me by my cousin and they lessened in importance. I confessed my own uncharitable thoughts. Time passed and the sun was warm on my head. I shuffled one arm out of my sweater sleeve. A noise clattered from below and I raised my eyes. I blinked several times. Was I dreaming again or was that really Tyler Livingstone crossing the sand in my direction, his black lunch pail swinging back and forth against his leg? If he was an apparition, he was a noisy one. As Tyler got closer, I made out the tune to "Magic Carpet Ride" as he hummed his way toward me. He was wearing heavy work boots, jeans, and a tan work shirt, and his brown hair swung loose around his face. Before starting to climb, he stuck his lunch pail on a piece of driftwood at the base of the rock hill.

"Hey, Darlene," he said as he settled next to me on the wide, flat surface of my rock. He smelled of shampoo and Irish Spring soap. He played an air guitar for a few minutes and sang in a low octave, "Let the sound take you away ...."

I shut my diary and slid it under my knee. Hadn't he figured out I was avoiding him? "You rock a mean Steppenwolf, Livingstone. Heading to work, or are you on your way to the tour bus?" I asked.

He dropped his hands and grinned. "Yeah. I'm early and thought I might find you here. Actually, I saw you walking this way when I was coming back from my jog. I remember we used to hang out on this rock and it was your favourite place. Took a chance."

"Since the time we were little and used to pretend we were explorers in a new world." I immediately regretted getting nostalgic. It wasn't a great way to get him thinking of me as having aged past twelve.

Tyler laughed. "You were always the one dreaming up the games. I just played along. I always wished I had half your imagination."

He was looking at me with his head tucked, stealing a glance to see if I'd gotten over whatever had made me mad the summer before. I hadn't spoken to him for most of July and the whole month of August, and wasn't sure he'd cared all that much since he'd spent the entire time with his new friends: Jane Ratherford and the in-crowd.

"How do you like working construction?" I asked.

"Sucks, to tell you the truth, but the money's okay."

"I can't believe you're out jogging before work."

"Hockey team tryouts come early. I want to make first line."

We sat silent for a bit, looking at the lake. I thought about the number of times I would relive this moment after he was gone. Tyler shifted forward and leaned on his elbows on his knees. "Your cousin ..."

"Elizabeth."

"Yeah, Elizabeth. Are you close?"

"Not really. I guess we'll be closer by the time the summer is over."

"You don't look alike."

"Yeah, Elizabeth gives thanks every day."

Tyler turned toward me. "I don't know. I always liked your red hair. Suits you."

"Thanks ... I think."

Tyler gave me a little push on my arm. "You gotta learn how to take a compliment, Dar. No wisecracks."

"Yeah, well, easy for you to say. Are you going to the beach party this weekend?"

Tyler stared at me like he wasn't going to let me off that easily. He stopped what he was about to say and looked out at the lake. "Probably. If I'm not too tired. I'm not used to working all day shovelling gravel. Uses a whole new set of muscles. Say, I saw the man that's living in the Davidson cottage for the summer. He was talking to your mom outside the store the other morning."

"Really? His name's Johnny Lewis. Mom probably was helping him out with something."

"They were still talking when I jogged by on my way back. I was surprised anyone else was up that early."

I shrugged as if I wasn't concerned. "Mom's an early riser."

Tyler started pushing himself into a standing position. "Well, my ride should be here in a few minutes, so I better get back to the road." He hesitated and looked over at me. "Do you come here every morning?"

"Usually."

"See you around sometime then."

"Yeah, see you around."

I watched him scramble down the rocks and bend to pick up his lunch pail before he started jogging down the beach. The shape of him and the way he moved were as familiar to me as breathing. I hit my forehead with the palm of my hand. Stupid. Stupid. Stupid. He only wanted me as a friend. He'd made that clear when he started up with Jane. It was even clearer now that he was checking out my beautiful cousin Elizabeth. I didn't know if I could bear Tyler being with Elizabeth, even if I never stood a chance of being his girlfriend. Compared to Tyler dating Jane Ratherford, him going out with Elizabeth would be like going from a paper cut to a leg amputation.

Mom met me at the front steps to the store. She looked harried, like she was late for something. "At last, there you are. Madelaine Brassard called and wants you to look after her baby around eleven. I'm going to town for a bit but will make sure I'm back in time to take over, if you watch the store for me while I'm gone."

"Are you sure you'll be back in time?"

"Yes. I won't be more than two hours."

I tried to meet her eyes but she had her head down and was digging around in her purse. "Okay," I said.

"Good. Maybe Elizabeth will help if you ask her." Mom gave me a quick smile before passing me on the steps.

Elizabeth would help me when we'd solved world hunger. I kept the thought from finding my mouth. No point making Mom crazy. I watched her back out of the driveway and then went inside. My first baby-sitting job and all I wanted to do was go over to visit

Candy and find out more about her exciting past. Being stuck in the store was a frustration piled on top of a lot of others.

I walked toward the kitchen to get something to eat. Elizabeth was sitting at the table lifting a spoonful of Cheerios to her mouth while reading the paper. She was wearing a square of cherry red scarf knotted loosely at the nape of her neck and a choker of blue and silver beads, the same colours in her tie-dyed tank top. She looked up at me. "Well, if it isn't the missing in action Darlene Findley. I hear you got a babysitting job today."

"Do you want to go, to make some money?" I asked.

"Well, I would, but I meant to tell you yesterday that your friend came by."

"Which friend?"

"The Chinese girl ... Michelle."

"I thought Michelle wasn't coming to the lake until later today."

"No, she had yesterday off and wanted you to go with her to Kingston this morning to pick up her boyfriend Danny. He lent her his car. Anyhow, she invited me and I said I'd love to go along for the ride and some shopping." Elizabeth bit her bottom lip. She looked uncertain. "If you'd rather go with Michelle, I can stay behind and babysit."

I looked at Elizabeth's bowed head. I weighed what would happen if I went and she didn't. "No, you go," I said. "Besides, I have to look after the store this morning while Mom goes into town."

Elizabeth's smile was a light turned on. "Thanks, Cuz. I'll take the next babysitting job, I promise."

"No problem." I took a bowl out of the cupboard and a spoon from the drawer and sat across from Elizabeth. I reached for the box of Cheerios. "Anything exciting in the news?" I asked.

"The Vietnam War is still going on. Big yawn. Looks like they're another step closer to giving eighteen-year-old Americans the vote. Carole King's record *Tapestry* got a good review."

"Did you follow that big anti-war demonstration in Washington in April?"

Elizabeth shook her head.

"The Americans should just get out of Vietnam. Especially after the My Lai massacre. I can't understand how those American soldiers could live with themselves after slaughtering an entire village." I was starting to sound like Gideon.

"Call back all those good-looking soldiers," said Elizabeth. "Maybe they should only send over soldiers older than thirty. I wonder if they've thought the draft through. You know, if the politicians who decided to go to war actually had to go there to fight, they might decide differently."

Her last sentence made some kind of weird sense. Maybe she wasn't so clueless. "What do you think of Richard Nixon?"

"He looks like a gnome, not somebody who should be president of the United States. He has a funny nose. I miss John F. Kennedy."

"Yeah, although I don't remember much about Kennedy except when he was assassinated. It was sort of the first time I started thinking about politics. I was in grade three when he was shot and I remember going home and crying because my mom was so sad. I hadn't even known there was a president before that or that the United States wasn't part of our country."

"I find politics boring, but Kennedy was much cuter than Nixon. The president should be good to look at. That should be part of the screening process. Look at Canada. We have Pierre Trudeau running the country and he's got women falling all over him."

So much for Elizabeth's insight. Her hormones were more active than her brain.

"Have you heard Carole King's record?" I asked.

Elizabeth's eyes brightened. "I love it. 'You've Got a Friend' is my favourite song on the album."

"Mine too."

At least we had something in common.

I turned as Michelle walked from the store into the kitchen. She was wearing patched bell bottoms and a navy and white striped T-shirt. Her black hair was pulled back into a ponytail.

"Hi, guys," she said. "Are you both coming to Kingston for the day?"

"Just me," said Elizabeth, jumping up and grabbing her jute purse from where it hung across the back of her chair. "See you later, Dar."

"I'm sorry you can't come," Michelle said to me. "It would have been fun."

Second Chances

"I'm sorry too." *You have no idea how sorry.*

"Maybe next time."

After they'd gone, I looked out the window for a bit and then stood up to dump the rest of my cereal into the garbage before I went upstairs to brush my teeth.

Chapter Five

THE BRASSARDS' BLUE cottage with yellow shutters was on the opposite side of the lake, past Gideon's place. I biked over just before lunch and found Madelaine waiting on the front steps with her friend, Susie Carmichael. They were heading to town to eat and didn't want to waste any time getting there. The baby, Cheryl, had already been put down for her nap and there was nothing for me to do but read magazines and watch *Take Thirty* followed by the afternoon movie on the black-and-white television in the beach-musty living room that smelled of Pledge and cigarette smoke. The movie was one of those Roman warrior ones with the men running around in tunics and the women all gorgeous and getting rescued. It wasn't a tough way to earn five dollars, but it was a boring one.

I walked around the inside of the cottage several times and only just stopped myself from waking up Cheryl, who turned out to be the sleeper of all sleepers. I even checked a few times to make certain she was breathing, leaning over the crib and putting my ear close to her nose. She finally woke up about twenty minutes before her mom came through the door. I was just warming up a bottle of milk in a pan of water on the stove. It was a relief to take the money and leave. I didn't want to become a mother anytime soon. The baby smell of dirty diapers, talcum powder, and milk made the air close and stifling and had given me a headache.

It was still early, so I stopped at Gideon's on my way past his house. I pedalled up his driveway, leaned my bike against the wall and wandered into the back yard. Gideon was sitting in front of the open window working on his typewriter. His grey hair was a swirl of fluff across the top of his head with thicker tufts around his ears. From where I stood in the grass, his face looked pasty and his cheeks droopy. Gideon must have sensed me there because he lifted his head and smiled in my direction, and suddenly he looked younger. He pulled the pipe out of his mouth and motioned for me to enter. Ruby met me at the door and nuzzled against my leg. I reached down and scratched behind her ears.

"Come right in, Darlene. Ruby girl, give our guest some walking room! Would you like something to drink, Little Fin?"

"I'll just get a glass of water, if that's okay."

"Help yourself. I'm just putting the finishing touches on my column."

I let the water run for a while until it was cold and then filled two glasses. I set one next to Gideon's typewriter and looked over his shoulder at the paper as his big nicotine-stained fingers hunted and pecked the keys, staccato time. "What's it about this week?"

Gideon grunted. "Why big business wants the Vietnam War to continue. How the United States and the western hemisphere have been suckered into fighting in a country we have no damn right to be in." He turned away from me and coughed. "Bloody cold. I'll be glad when I shake it."

"I hate war."

"You and every other person with an ounce of brains. Have you been managing to get some writing in?"

"Uh-huh." I sat in Gideon's easy chair and he swivelled around to face me. His eyes searched my face.

"You look a little down. Anything you want to talk about?"

"I'm okay. Just the normal teenage stuff, you know: Why is my hair red? When will I get a date? When does the exciting part start?"

"It's a rocky road, no way around that. Patience, Little Fin. Patience. All things unfold as they should. Is your father coming for the weekend?"

"Dad should be here around suppertime. Mom's cooking a big meal."

Gideon nodded and smiled. "I saw your mom in town this morning having coffee in Downy's. She's one helluva woman, your mama."

I think I hid my surprise. It wasn't about her being special, but the coffee part. Dad said having coffee in a restaurant was a waste of money and Mom went along with him.

"She wanted a break from the store," I said.

"I can see that," Gideon nodded. "It must be nice for that young man to have a friend like your mom, being new to the lake and all. He looks like someone who keeps to himself. Being around your mother makes people shine."

My heart started beating funny and I wouldn't look Gideon in the face. I had a feeling I knew who he was talking about and it wasn't good. Not good at all. I sipped my water and spilled some down the front of my shirt. The shock of cold made me gasp.

Gideon had turned back around. "Do you want to read what I've got written so far?" His pulled the page out of the typewriter. "You can tell me if I've broken down into more of a rant than usual."

"Sure."

I took the pages from him. I wasn't an expert, but I liked nothing better than working with Gideon on a piece of writing. It would take my mind off my mother and her coffee date. It would keep Gideon from reading what was written on my face.

By the time I got home, Dad was sitting in the kitchen with the newspaper spread out in front of him on the table. Mom was making supper while keeping an eye out for any customers.

"There you are," said Mom. "How was babysitting?"

"Good." I grabbed an apple from the fruit bowl. I couldn't look at her. "Hi, Dad."

"Hello, Darlene." Dad lifted his head and nodded at me then looked back down at what he was reading. His work shirt was draped across the back of his chair and he was dressed in his undershirt. He kept speaking with his head down. "Your mother could use some help."

Are your hands broken? The thought popped into my head. I looked away so he wouldn't read in my eyes what I was thinking. "What would you like me to do, Mom?" I asked to keep myself from saying something I'd regret.

"If you watch the store until I get these vegetables going, that would be perfect."

I looked at Mom then, I mean really looked, trying to see her as Gideon did ... and Johnny Lewis too. She was five foot five with shoulder length brown hair, today tied back in a ponytail. Slim with curves that I hoped to inherit some day; a wide mouth and warm eyes the colour of nutmeg. There were lines around her eyes and mouth that deepened when she smiled or frowned. I'd always found it easy to read my mother's moods, but she'd become preoccupied lately, and her distance made me lonely. I wanted it to go back to the way it had been between us. I didn't know how to get there. She saw me watching her and questioned me with her eyes.

"Did you ... I mean, how did it go in town?" I asked. Dad raised his head. For a split second, Mom's eyes flashed alarm, but when she spoke, her voice was even.

"Good. I just ran into the store and out." She turned to my father and raised her hands waist high, palms spread as she explained. "I wanted to surprise you with the roast."

Dad grunted. "I could have picked it up on my way. There wasn't any need for you to go into town, price of gas what it is."

"I know, but I wanted to."

"You've no sense sometimes, woman," he grumbled, but that seemed to satisfy him. He lowered his head to read. Mom's eyes dismissed me before she turned her back and started stirring something in a pot on the stove.

What have I done? I felt like she'd slapped me but this was way worse. I crept away without saying anything more. I closed the door between the shop and our kitchen. It took me a while to cross the shop and sit on the stool behind the counter. I was having trouble getting my feet to move forward, and my stomach had something fluttering around inside trying to get out. *What have I done? She wouldn't even look at me.* I told myself it didn't matter, but I knew it did. Mom and I had always stood together, a unit of two keeping each other safe from my father and his fears and anger. I knew exactly what I had done. *I'd betrayed her.*

The front door opened. Four kids coming in to buy popsicles — two banana, a cherry, and a grape. I forgot to hand one boy his change and he banged on the counter until I dropped coins into his hand. They left and I paced around the floor for a while before grabbing a magazine and returning to my stool. I started flipping through it, the same *Mad* magazine I'd picked up the week before, when I'd first seen Tyler Livingstone. The words were blurry and I wiped my eyes with the back of my hand. The bell jingled, and I glanced up.

Candy Parsens was walking towards me, a big smile on her face, hair tied back with wispy bits hanging loose around her face. Her tight red T-shirt had a dark stain across the right side of her stomach, and her wrinkled white peasant skirt trailed in a crooked line above her bare feet, blackened with a coat of mud. The pupils of her eyes were dilated. Her fluttering hands mesmerized me, darting back and forth in front of her like a couple of baby birds. I straightened up.

"Where's Sean?" I asked, worried.

Candy waved a pale hand toward the front window. "Kid's home. Just came for some ciggies." She squinted at me. "Darlene? That *is* you." She frowned. "You didn't come by and I waited all afternoon."

"I was going to go see you but it was raining. Is Sean home with Johnny?"

"We could have gone swimming in the rain. Wet's wet." Candy laughed, loud and high-pitched. It ended suddenly when she drew in her breath and pointed with a trembling finger to the red du Maurier package of cigarettes behind the counter. Her face got serious. She reminded me of a kid trying to be good. "Come by tomorrow if you can, say after lunch sometime." She slapped two Crispy Crunches on the counter and spun around to take a large bag of barbecue chips from the shelf. She staggered and grabbed onto the top of the display, crunching bags of chips with her weight. Then she spun back around and waved her hand in the air. "Damn blackflies," she said. "I can't get away from them."

"I don't see any," I said.

"Well, are you coming for that swim? We can go right now!"

"I have to watch the store. I'll try tomorrow," I said, more to get her to stop talking about it than because I thought I'd go. I looked toward the back of the store. All I would need was for one of my parents to walk in and hear me agreeing to go swimming with her. I put her stuff into a paper bag and slid it across the counter. She threw in two packs of gum that she'd taken from the display. I rang everything into the register. "Two dollars and ten cents."

"Call it a babysitting job, you know, when you come. I'll pay you to watch Seany while I swim. It'll be good to have you. It gets lonely there all day by myself."

"I'll try to come after lunch."

Candy reached in slow motion into the pocket of her skirt and pulled out a lighter. Her face puckered. "Damn! I forgot my money. Can I pay you tomorrow?"

"Mom doesn't let ... "

"That's okay. I'm good for it."

Candy grabbed the bag and had tucked it against her hip as if she was carrying a baby. Her eyes drifted past mine and focused on the dust particles dancing in the late afternoon sunlight streaming in through the window. She moved toward the door and I didn't know how to stop her.

"You can pay me tomorrow when I come babysit," I called.

Now I'll have to go see you.

"You're an angel. A beautiful little red-haired angel." Candy waved at me and stepped through the door.

She let the screen door snap shut, and I moved in front of the window to watch her trip down the path toward the road. She looked ghostly in her white skirt and floating steps, almost dancing into the trees, her hair flowing behind her like golden ribbons. I watched until she had disappeared from view before going back to my seat on the stool behind the counter. I stared back toward the window and tried to make my eyes focus on a story in the magazine, but all I kept thinking about was Candy leaving Sean alone in the house.

A few minutes later, a car door slammed. I lifted my head. Elizabeth bounded into the store. She was carrying a shopping bag, and she was smiling. "That was a great day," she said. "Too bad you decided not to come."

I pretended it had been my choice to stay. "What did you buy?"

"A few tops and the best pair of black clogs. It wasn't Toronto, but it was good to get into a mall again. It was like … like there is life after Cedar Lake." She took a few steps and turned around. "Michelle and Danny will meet us at the beach around nine. Is that okay?"

"I guess I can fit it in."

I watched Elizabeth saunter through the store and enter the kitchen, letting the door swing closed behind her. Her voice mingled with my parents'. My father's low rumble seemed to go on a long time. Elizabeth said something I couldn't make out and my father laughed.

A burning feeling started in my stomach and worked its way up. I crumpled up the magazine and flung it against the wall with all my might. It made a satisfying thunk when it hit. I lowered my arm and laid it across the counter, then rested my cheek in the crook of my elbow. I stayed that way until the bell jingled and a customer came in to buy milk.

"I'll catch up with you at the beach," I said to Elizabeth. "Dad wants me to stock shelves before I go. We have tins of cat food that need urgent stacking. Code red. Cats won't sleep soundly tonight unless the Findley shelves are full of Puss n' Boots."

We were in the bedroom getting ready for the beach party.

"You should stand up for yourself and tell him where he can put the cat food," said Elizabeth, leaning into the mirror to put another layer of mascara on her lashes. "What are you, his bloody slave?" Her eyes found mine in the glass.

I stretched my arms to the ceiling and pulled a clean T-shirt over my head. It was dark green and scoop-necked and fit me better than most tops I owned. It made my eyes look greener than usual and my chest bigger, or I liked to think so.

"My father is obsessed with making me a productive member of society. If I tell him where he can stuff the cat food, I'd better be running for the door because if he ever caught me, I'd be eating a few cans."

Elizabeth spun around. Her eyes had narrowed. "Has he ... would he ever hit you or anything?"

"No. My father doesn't hit."

"Good, because that would just be sick." She patted her hair then straightened her new black T-shirt that was cropped above her belly button. "So, how do I look?"

"Great. I like your top." I turned toward the door. "I think I hear Mom calling you."

Elizabeth went into the hallway and leaned over the banister. "Yes, Aunt Jan?" she yelled.

I couldn't hear the answer Mom sent up the stairs but heard Elizabeth say, "Phone's for me. See you later." Her feet clattered down the stairs double time in her new clogs.

I followed her down at a slower pace as I wove my good leather belt through the loops of my jeans. I'd just finished buckling it when I reached the kitchen. Elizabeth was leaning against the wall with one hand cupped over the phone receiver, her back toward me. She didn't see me waiting in the doorway.

"Have you eaten today? You still have to eat even if he doesn't come home. No, Mom? Mom? Are you still there? Stop crying…. Just go to bed, all right?" Her voice dropped. "You've got to start taking care of yourself. It doesn't matter if he doesn't come home."

I left then, walking as quietly as I could through the kitchen and keeping an eye on Elizabeth to see if she turned around. I stepped inside the store and started breathing again. *What was going on with my aunt and uncle?* I jumped when my father's voice boomed across the room.

"There you are. I let your mother go for a walk and

said I'd close tonight. Come on. Let's get these cans on the shelves."

"Sure, Dad."

We worked side by side in silence. Every so often, Dad would point at one of the cans I'd placed on the shelf, and I'd adjust it so the label was facing forward or move the can so that they were all perfectly spaced. He kept going into the storage room and bringing out boxes of canned stuff. Soup, waxed beans, ravioli, spaghetti sauce, stewed tomatoes, corn, fruit in syrup. We worked steadily and silently for over an hour. Every time I thought we were done, Dad would get up and go find some more boxes.

"How's your summer going?" he asked after his last trip to the storage room. His voice took on a formal tone like it did whenever we were alone together.

"Good so far."

"Your mother tells me William will be here next weekend."

"I haven't seen him since Christmas. I wish I could have gone with Mom to Toronto when she went to visit him."

I clamped my mouth shut. I'd forgotten Dad hadn't wanted her to go. She'd taken the bus four times since last summer to see William, and Dad had tried to talk her out of it every time. He'd roamed the house half the night when she was gone. Said he couldn't sleep with her away.

Dad grunted. "Your brother has his own life now. Your mother has to accept that. He'll come home if he wants to see us."

I bit my bottom lip to keep from saying something that would provoke him. "Anything else, Dad?"

"No, looks like we're done here. You can head out. I expect you to be on your best behaviour and take care of your cousin."

"Yes, sir." I walked quickly to the front door before he changed his mind and made me alphabetize something or start lining up chocolate bars.

I met Mom near the road. She was just starting up the path. Her face in the full moon's light was silvery. She was holding buttercups and daisies in front of her like a bridal bouquet. She reminded me of a fairy in *A Midsummer Night's Dream*, my favourite Shakespeare play by a long shot. I was glad she couldn't see my face clearly.

"Are you off to the beach?" she asked. "Isn't Elizabeth going with you?"

"She's already there. I stayed to help Dad."

"Ah yes. The replenishing of the shelves. Thanks for that. I needed a break."

From the store or from Dad? "Were you alone all this time?" I asked.

"Yes."

"Maybe next time, I can watch the store and Dad can go with you."

Mom laughed. "Now when has your father ever wanted to go for a walk with no destination? He'd much rather stay home and watch television or read the paper."

She had me there. "Well, I better get going. There won't be any beer left if I'm much later."

"Darlene ... "

"Just kidding, Mom."

"Sometimes you worry me. If you say something flip around your father.... Well, you know he worries about you and doesn't have a sense of humour when it comes to what you might get into."

"I know. I'll be careful."

Mom stepped closer and gave me a hug. "He does love you," she whispered. "He just worries so much." She kissed my forehead and brushed my hair out of my eyes before letting me go and continuing up the path.

I turned to watch her until she climbed the steps and disappeared into the store. I kept walking toward the beach with a question stuck in my mind that I tried to hum away. I couldn't quite manage it, but even if my mother'd been standing in front of me at that very moment, I still wouldn't have found the courage to ask why her hair smelled of cigarettes when she told me she'd been all alone on her walk.

I circled the crowd until I found Michelle, Danny, and Elizabeth sitting on a log near the water. Danny had an arm slung over Michelle's shoulders and they were listening to Elizabeth. She must have said something funny because they all burst out laughing as I got closer. She was turning into quite the comedian. I dropped down next to Danny.

"At last," said Michelle. "We were starting to think you weren't coming."

Danny took a bottle of beer from a small cooler sitting at his feet and snapped off the lid with a bottle opener. He handed the bottle to me. "You look like you could use one." He bumped against my arm. "How's it going? We missed you today."

I turned toward him. "Okay. Made five whole dollars babysitting. How's the ice cream business?"

"You know, it's a job. I'm digging your cousin. She's got a great sense of humour."

"Does she?" The words were out before I thought about how they sounded. "I don't think she likes cottage life," I added.

"Understandable. It's good of her though, you know. Toughing it out for the summer. Can't be easy."

"What do you mean?"

"Come on, Darlene. She's given up her lifestyle in TO, a boyfriend and all her friends to come stay with a family she barely knows in the middle of nowhere. You should really cut her some slack, you know."

"What's she been saying?"

Danny's shoulder rubbed up and down against mine in a shrug. "Not much, but it doesn't take a genius to read between the lines."

"Yeah, we've been working her like a dog. She barely has time to lie in the hammock and read or go to Kingston with *my* friends."

"Come on, Darlene. If you keep excluding her, she's going to find other ways to keep busy."

I looked over at the person who was ruining my life. Elizabeth and Michelle had their heads close together, talking about something of obvious importance. Every so often they laughed like they were the two most amusing people on the beach. Elizabeth's face was glowing in the firelight. She didn't look lonely or left out to me. Why was I the only one who saw through her act? I raised the beer bottle to my lips. My face felt flushed and I took a deep pull, letting the beer fill my mouth and travel down my throat to drown the bad feeling rising up from my stomach. I tuned in Danny mid-sentence.

"... to quit our jobs mid-August and hitchhike to Vancouver. Michelle has a lot of family living on the mainland and Vancouver Island who we can stay with. It'll be a good break before school starts."

"Her parents won't care if the two of you go on a trip alone together?" I asked.

"She hasn't asked them yet, but we're trying to get a few more people to come. Interested?"

"Probably not. I have to help Mom in the store."

"Oh yeah, the store. Well, maybe next year."

"Yeah, maybe."

I looked across at my cousin. She was dancing across the sand toward us, swinging her hips back and forth and rotating her stomach like a belly dancer. Her hair swirled around her as she spun in a circle. She ended up behind us and bent down to put her arms around Danny's and my shoulders. "What are you two so serious about? This is a party! Come on, let's dance."

She pulled Danny by the arm to his feet and dragged him closer to the fire. He pretended to resist at first, then held up his hands in mock surrender. They began moving their feet in time to the radio, which was thumping out "Bad Moon Rising."

I looked across at Michelle. She was watching Danny and Elizabeth with a big smile on her face, but her eyes looked like somebody had just given her some very bad news. I grabbed two beers out of the cooler and moved next to her on the log, knocking against her leg with mine.

"So what did you buy in Kingston?" I moved closer so she'd have to look at me and not my cousin and Danny.

"Just the Rod Stewart album, *Every Picture Tells a Story*. He does that song 'Maggie May.' Ever heard it?"

I shook my head.

"The album just came out in May. I'll play it for you some time. I really wish you'd come with us."

"Next time, hopefully. Mom needs my help with William gone. I'm beginning to realize how much he did in the store. This is the first summer he hasn't spent a few months at the lake. Say, do you want to go talk to Penny Rogers? I see her over there." I pointed to a group of girls at the far end of the beach.

"Let's go." Michelle stood up and grabbed my arm. She'd had more beer than I'd realized. We circled the fire and walked across the sand, past the small group dancing. Now Elizabeth was slow waltzing with Danny. I tried to block Michelle's view. She saw anyway and lurched hard against me.

Phil and Greg, two of Tyler's friends, were strumming guitars near the water. Tyler was sitting beside them watching Jane Ratherford and a couple of her friends dancing barefoot in the sand. Tyler had his head back drinking from a beer bottle, and by the look on his face and the way he was leaning, appeared to already have had several. The sweet smell of weed drifted our way. I waved as I passed by them and kept walking toward the path, holding Michelle upright.

"I think I just want to go home," Michelle said as we neared Penny's group. "Not feeling so great."

"I'll walk you." I was glad for any excuse to leave. I wouldn't be coming back.

Chapter Six

THE NEXT AFTERNOON, Elizabeth was just getting out of bed when I ran upstairs to get my bathing suit. I'd been sound asleep when she'd come home from the party.

"How'd it go last night?" I asked her as I rifled through my top drawer to find a hair elastic.

"Great! Where did you disappear to so early?"

"You were busy dancing, and Michelle wasn't feeling so great, so I took her home. After that, I just came home too."

"Too bad. You and Michelle missed a good time." Elizabeth flipped back her hair and stretched her arms over her head. She was sitting on the side of her bed, dressed in pink baby doll pajamas. "We're going to see a movie — *Cactus Flower* — in Campbellford later this afternoon ... at least, Danny and I decided to go. I'm not sure about Michelle yet. Danny said he'd ask her this morning." Elizabeth pouted and flicked a hand in the air as if she was tossing away Michelle.

"I saw that movie last year in Ottawa," I said. "If you like Goldie Hawn, you'll enjoy it." My new being pleasant tactic seemed to be working. No more rising to her bait. I began to hum.

Elizabeth nodded. After a few seconds, her eyes focused on mine. "Oh, here's something that might interest you. I spent quite a bit of time talking to your friend Tyler last night. He's very funny and *sooo* interesting." She was watching me, her Mona Lisa smile pasted on.

"I'm glad you're getting along with my friends," I said carefully. I picked up my hair brush and an elastic band and slammed the drawer shut. "I'm off to another babysitting job. Have fun at the movie."

"Have fun babysitting. Danny and I will be meeting up with Tyler after the movie when he's done work. I'll say hello for you."

I stopped smiling and stared at her.

Elizabeth pushed herself out of bed and pulled her top over her head with one swift motion, arching her back and flashing her naked breasts in my direction. They were perfectly round and about the size of small grapefruits with pointy brown nipples. The tan line from her bikini showed how her skin had darkened to a mocha colour in the sun. She was slender and her waist curved in just a bit over her narrow hips.

I averted my eyes as she strutted past me to the door. I looked in the mirror at my own pale skin and the freckles on my arms and spread across my forehead and cheeks.

"Just off for a shower," Elizabeth said, swinging her pajama top across her chest as she stepped into the hall.

"I'll tell you all about my adventure when I get back."

I waited until I heard her enter the bathroom and the door closing before I followed her out of the bedroom.

There was another car in Candy's driveway — a black four-door Chevy with a New York licence plate, the side panels covered in dried mud and the windshield splattered with dead bugs. The car looked like it had been driven over some nasty back roads. I wondered who'd come visiting.

Loud guitar music led me down the path and around the house to the back yard. I looked toward the back of the property. Candy was sitting on a blanket under the oak tree with Sean running around in front of her. He was wearing a saggy diaper and nothing else. His mouth looked like he'd taken a bite out of a mud pie.

I didn't see the two men facing away from me in lawn chairs at the edge of the patio until I was halfway across the grass. I lifted a hand in a quick wave. They were both watching me but neither waved back. I felt awkward knowing they were staring at me as I walked toward Candy. The smaller one started to get up until his friend said something that I couldn't hear and motioned for him to sit down.

I focused on Candy. She looked pretty in a flowery yellow dress that reached her ankles and billowed around her in the breeze off the lake. She smiled when she saw me and patted the blanket next to her. I made it the last few steps and lowered myself down beside her. I couldn't see her eyes behind the round oversized sunglasses that dwarfed her face and made her look like a kid playing dress-up. The two men were now facing me and they each mouthed hello as Candy pointed in their direction. I was having trouble hearing what she was saying over Hendrix's guitar wailing from the speakers that aimed out through the open kitchen windows. Luckily, the needle scratched at the end of the record as she finished her introductions.

"… meet Bobby and Kirk, his brother. They've come all the way from Jersey to visit." They each nodded at me when she said their names.

Bobby and Kirk didn't resemble each other much. Bobby had a dirty blonde Afro and a full beard. He was the one who'd been about to stand up when he'd seen me. His eyes were close-set and he had the look of someone squinting through a fog. He was wearing a red and blue striped poncho that looked dirty around the edges. Kirk was taller and heavier with a crew cut and the bottom of an eagle tattoo showing from under his black t-shirt. His arm rippled like water as he flexed his muscles. He looked smarter than Bobby by a long shot. They were both holding brown beer bottles. Bobby took a few swallows and then rubbed the back of his hand across his mouth. A trail of the white foam dribbled down his beard.

"Hi there," said Kirk. His smile should have been friendly, but it didn't come across that way. He reached into his pocket and pulled out some aviator sunglasses. He slid them on his face in a quick motion. They hid something in his eyes that had made the hairs on my arms stand up.

"Are you here for a visit?" I asked. Being polite to adults was so ingrained, they could have been axe murderers and I'd have asked them if they were enjoying the sights.

"Just thought we'd hang out with our good 'ol friends for a while," said Kirk. "What time did you say Johnny would be home?"

I felt Candy shift positions beside me. "I don't expect him until five. If you all want to drive into town to get that tequila you were talking about, don't let me keep you."

Bobby was looking at Candy like she had something he wanted. He lifted a hand trying to get her attention. Candy kept her eyes on Kirk. Time skipped a few beats.

"Yeah, we could do that." Kirk stood up. "Come on, Bobby. Let's split for a while."

Bobby stood too, but not in any big hurry. He kept staring at Candy until he had to turn his back to walk with Kirk away from us. They disappeared around the side of the house.

"Who are they?" I asked.

Candy shrugged. "People that Johnny knows from the States. Nobody important. They'll probably be here a week or so."

"Bobby seems to like you."

"You noticed too, huh?" She grinned.

Sean was trying to catch Candy's attention. He was spinning around the yard and squealing in a high-pitched screech. His diaper sagged so low that I thought he would lose it. I gagged when he got close to me. Candy ignored him and lay back on the blanket.

"What a glorious day. I just love it here. I could lie on the grass grooving in the sunshine forever. Such a good change from New York City. You have no idea."

I wrapped my arms around my legs and rested a cheek against my knee. "Did Johnny go into town?" I asked.

"Johnny? Yeah. He had some things to do in Toronto, so no worry about him showing up soon."

It wasn't what I meant. In fact, I wanted to meet him, to find out what he had going on with my mom. "What does Johnny do?"

"Oh, this and that. I try not to get involved in his business. It bores me silly. Chasing the almighty dollar is a waste of your life. I'd rather spend my days outside, enjoying the day, communing with nature." She smiled at me. "What do you like to do?"

"I help my mom in the store quite a bit or I read, swim, you know, the regular stuff. I like to write."

"A writer?" She squealed. "I should have known! You have that deep, mysterious way about you. I knew some writers in my old life. Have you ever heard of J.D. Salinger?"

"The *Catcher in the Rye* Salinger? Of course! How did you know him? I heard he's a recluse."

Candy smiled. "A while back, you know, before I met up with Johnny, I made a pilgrimage to Cornish, New Hampshire, where he lives. He and his wife Claire had just separated. We spent several lovely days ... and nights together."

"He'd be a lot older than you, I guess."

"It didn't matter at the time. I drifted back to New

York City, though. I missed the people and the action in the big city."

"Wow. You've had an exciting life. I've never been far from Ottawa or met anyone famous."

Candy patted my leg. "You will someday. I can tell. There's something special about you that radiates just like sunshine. It's part of why I like you. Say, I'd love to read something that you've written. I'll bet it's good. Better than good."

I'd only shared my writing with Gideon and hadn't thought about letting anyone else read it. "Maybe I could let you read a poem that Gideon likes. He's kind of my mentor."

"Right on. I'd like that. Tell you what," said Candy. "Sean is ready for a nap, so you can come with me for a swim and I'll still pay you for looking after him. It's so nice to have someone to talk to."

"Are you sure we should leave him alone? I don't mind staying here and watching him."

Her voice hardened. "Sean will be fine. Once he's asleep, it takes a rocket to wake him up. We'll have an hour at least."

"If you're sure."

"I wouldn't leave him if I wasn't sure."

The water was cold and I couldn't stand being in it for long, but it didn't bother Candy. I paddled around for a bit and then found a flat rock on the beach that had baked in the sun. I wrapped myself in a beach towel and watched her swim to the little rock island and back. She was a strong swimmer. I dozed off and when I opened my eyes, she was running along the sand at the edge of the water in her bright, pink-flowered bikini, arms spread wide, thick wet hair trailing down her back and calling to me, "Come on in! The water's great."

"Shouldn't we be getting back? Sean might wake up," I called.

Candy stopped and shrugged. "In a while. It's early yet."

"I could go check on him."

"Really, you don't need to. I'm not kidding when I say he sleeps for two hours every afternoon. Kid's up most of the night." Her mouth clamped into a straight line. She crossed her arms across her chest and glared at me.

"Okay," I said.

She smiled at me again, as if I'd given her my blessing, then turned and splashed her way into the deeper water. My stomach tightened when I saw her heading out to the island a second time, her arms slicing through the water in steady strokes. I wondered if Sean had woken up yet and was crying for someone to come get him. The sun went behind a cloud. I shivered, wrapping the towel more tightly around my shoulders and willing Candy to come back. I waited another half hour before she got tired of swimming. She was still drying herself off with a beach towel when I told her I was late and had to get home to help my mom.

I walked through the back door and heard my father's angry voice, rising and falling like wind in the trees. I wanted to turn and run, but he would be alone with my mother and she'd be taking the brunt of his anger. I stepped inside the kitchen. Sure enough, Mom was sitting beside him at the table, her face blank, appearing to be listening while her body language told me she'd tuned him out. When she noticed me standing in the doorway, she motioned with her eyes for me to disappear up the back stairs, but my father saw her shifting expression and turned to spot me where I stood rooted in the doorway. His forehead glistened with sweat and a streak of grease blackened his cheek.

"There you are, Darlene. It's about time you showed up home. Your mother and I were just discussing how little help you are around here — always scribbling away in some book or nowhere to be found. It's time you pitched in more. I'm going to clean up from fixing that bloody washing machine, which took my whole bloody afternoon, and then I'm taking your mother to town for supper before I head back to Ottawa. You'll be in charge of the store until closing. No slouching off."

"I didn't know it was broken."

"Pardon me?"

"The washing machine. I didn't know it was broken."

My father's face pulsed purplish red and his voice rose a few pitches. "Of course you didn't. That would have meant you actually did some laundry or some work around here. Your school marks are average and you can't do anything right around the house. All I ask is that you take some of the load off your mother." He pounded the table with his fist and the salt and pepper shakers jumped. "And enough of your smartass talking back. I didn't know it was broken. Christ."

"I didn't mean ..."

Mom gave him a hard look as she cut me off. "There's a casserole I got ready for lunch tomorrow, but you can have it for supper. I'm not sure when Elizabeth will be back from town, but there's plenty for her to heat up later."

Dad took a deep breath, mumbled something, and stood up. He shook his head while he unhooked his suspenders and walked over to the sink, where he began washing his arms with dish detergent. Mom nodded at me and pointed to the store with a slight movement of her head. I started walking as quietly as I could to the door leading to the shop. As I passed her, she grabbed my arm and said quietly, "I don't know what I would do without you. He's just ... had a bad afternoon. A migraine and then the washing machine."

I didn't say anything back, but the anxiety in my throat eased a bit. Dad might not have heard me over the running water if I responded to my mother's comment, but I didn't want to take the chance of getting her in trouble. I straightened my shoulders and walked a little taller into the shop.

It was nearly seven o'clock and I was making my last circuit of the store to tidy shelves before locking up for the night. A rush of cottagers had kept me busy until around six thirty, but it had been quiet for the last ten minutes, and I was ready to get outside while there was still sunshine. I reached the cereal section and picked up a box of Rice Krispies that had fallen onto the floor. I was putting it on the shelf when the bell jangled on the front door. I peeked over the jars of pickles and nearly swallowed my gum.

Johnny Lewis was standing near the counter looking around. He was dressed in a white shirt and blue jeans and his black curls were pulled back into a short ponytail. He'd begun growing a beard and it made him look even better than the first time I'd seen him. My eyes dropped to his bare feet then back up to his face. His eyes got a little less shiny when I stepped out from behind the shelves.

"Your mother not working tonight?" he asked real casual-like. He picked up a pack of gum from the carton and flipped it end on end in his hand while he looked at me with his Al Pacino eyes.

"She's out with my dad for supper," I said. "They do lots of things together." I skirted around him and got behind the counter. "Dad wanted to take my mother somewhere so she wouldn't have to cook. He says she's been working too hard lately." I said it all without taking a breath.

"Well, that's nice," Johnny said, looking at me with a half-smile on his face. His eyes looked amused. "She deserves a night away. I'll just buy this gum for Candy and a pack of cigs for me." He pointed to the green Export A pack on a ledge behind the counter.

I grabbed one and set it in front of him. "How do you like Cedar Lake? I'll bet you can't wait to get out of here and go back to Toronto for good."

"This is a great spot. I never liked living in the city much."

There was a hint of an accent in his voice. I looked down at his hands. They were tanned and rough-looking, and his nails were bitten down and jagged.

"Where did you live before?"

"Toronto the last while." His eyes softened and he grinned, looking way younger and friendly. "I understand you live in Ottawa when you're not here at the lake."

No wonder my mother liked him. The way he looked made me jumpy inside. My hands felt awkward, like they belonged to somebody else. I wondered what he and my mother talked about when they were together.

Whether he kissed her.

"We have a big house and Dad works in the mill. Mom inherited this store."

"When I was a kid, we used to come to Cedar Lake in the summers. It was way before your time."

"Did you know my mother then?"

"I was younger than her by a few years, but yeah, who wouldn't remember your mother?"

The way he said it made me feel a flush crawling up my cheeks, and I moved over to the cash register to ring in his sale. If I met Tyler Livingstone twenty years from now, would I feel something too, especially if I was married to someone like my father? I reached out to give Johnny his change. My fingers brushed against his skin and I felt a tingle that went up my wrist. *What the hell is wrong with me?*

Maybe Dad had sensed something between Johnny

and Mom, because he never took her out for supper when we were at the lake. He preferred she cook for him. He liked to say why waste money on restaurants when you could get a perfectly good meal at home. The truth was so far from what I'd just told Johnny that I felt sad.

"So, you grew up in Toronto then?" I asked. "You don't sound Canadian."

The expression in his eyes disappeared like he was shutting down inside, but he answered my question without any less friendliness in his voice. "Lived in South Carolina when I was a boy. My family spent summers here with my relatives. Your mom and her sister Peg spent summers here too." He grabbed the cigarettes and gum. "Thanks and give your mom my best."

He was near the door. I called out, "Mom told me you grew up in New York."

His shoulders tensed before he swung around and looked at me. "Yeah, that's right. We lived in New York after South Carolina. Manhattan to be exact."

"Your accent isn't as strong as Candy's."

Johnny studied me. "She spent more time in the South than I did. I got out first chance I could. Well, I guess I'll see you around."

"Yeah, see you around."

He pushed open the door and stepped outside, letting the screen door snap hard like a gunshot against the frame. He was gone so fast, he didn't look back to apologize. It was almost as if something had spooked him.

Chapter Seven

I CROSSED THE BEACH and climbed until I reached the refuge of my flat rock. Tonight, I'd brought my poetry notebook. I propped my back against the rock behind my seat and bent my knees so that I could write with my book resting against my legs. I'd been working on a poem inspired by my father.

> *I am not the person you see*
> *When your eyes meet mine*
> *I am more*
> *Than the broken pieces*
> *You've formed in your mind*

The start seemed okay, but I was struggling with the last line. I wasn't too sure about the word formed, but would let it stay for a while until I could think of something better. I looked out at the water.

Who did my father see when he looked at me? Was it me or my sister Annie? I used to think he got the two of us confused in his head, especially before he had the breakdown. He'd sit and stare at me when he thought I wasn't watching, as if he was trying to see something in my face that should have been there.

It was early evening in Ottawa. I was eight years old, sitting on the living room floor playing with my paper dolls. Dad had been in his recliner reading the paper as he did every night after supper. For some reason, I'd turned and looked up from where I'd organized my dolls on the couch. It might have been the sound of the paper dropping to the floor or the heaviness of his grief filling the room that made me raise my eyes to look at him. I remember not being able to take in what was happening at first, and then the fear that kept me rooted in place as if my arms and legs were frozen.

Tears silently tracked down my father's face in two straight lines. His shoulders heaved back and forth as if his whole body were going to come apart. I could feel my heart pounding hard in my chest where I sat as still as a mouse, trying to disappear into myself, but I jumped when a whimpering started deep in his throat. It rose in pitch to a keening, like a dog I'd seen once with its foot caught in a rabbit trap when William took me for a walk in the woods. The sound scared me so much that I sprang up from the carpet and ran for the door. I opened my mouth to call for my mother, but she was there before I made a sound. She'd flown past me into the living room, wiping her hands on her apron and calling my dad's name over and over. She'd dropped onto her knees beside his chair. I stood in the doorway until she yelled at me to go find William.

The ambulance came when I was skipping outside on the sidewalk. I stopped and watched two men dressed in white take Dad away strapped down on a stretcher. Mom followed with a look on her face I never wanted to see again.

When she got home from the hospital, I was in bed. She climbed the stairs to my room to check on me. I asked if Dad was okay, and she said he would be in time. For now, it was better if we didn't visit him in the hospital. She told William and me later that we shouldn't talk about Annie or Dad being sick after he came home. It was the last time I asked my mother about his breakdown. It was the start of our silent pact to pretend that Annie had never existed.

I sat on my rock, listening to the waves breaking on the beach and watching the sun sink lower and start to light up the horizon in faint pink that deepened into orange and black. Every so often, I'd close my eyes and let myself drift off. The mosquitoes and blackflies were making their nightly visit, but I'd brought a hooded sweatshirt that I pulled on over my head. I tightened the strings around my neck so that they couldn't get into my hair and hunkered down to wait them out. Once the sun went down completely, they'd be gone wherever it is flies go to sleep. I sat there on my rock until the rim of the sun disappeared and the moon took over, sparkling light across the water and the sand. I liked being at the beach when it was dark. The whole world took on a mystical feel and I felt part of something bigger than myself. Less alone.

I must have dozed off because I didn't hear his approach until he was on the rock below me. I almost tumbled sideways off my ledge.

"Not scared to be out here all by yourself after dark?"

I clutched where my heart was trying to break through my chest. "Not until this exact moment, I wasn't. What are you doing here?"

"I just like sitting here with you on this rock."

Tyler swung a blue-jeaned leg up over and turned himself around so he was next to me. His leg touched mine, he was sitting that close. I wondered if my heart would ever slow down, but I knew I was being stupid. He'd chosen Jane Ratherford over me the summer before. He didn't want me for a girlfriend and I didn't want to be anything but. An angry part of me wished he'd just leave me alone. The bigger part of me was glad he'd come.

"What're you writing?" he asked. He'd picked up my notebook and let the first page fall open. I grabbed it from him and tucked it under my bum.

"Just some poetry I'm playing around with. Nothing worth reading."

"Maybe you can read me something."

"It's too dark."

"Yeah." Tyler sighed and leaned back against the big rock behind us. His voice got real soft. "Do you miss Cedar Lake when you're away for the winter?"

"Yeah," I said. "Hard to believe, I know. There's never much going on here, but I feel ... I don't know ... free or something when I'm at the lake."

"I know what you mean. I guess you have to come here from the time you're little to get it. Remember all the fun you and me had? It would be nice if things hadn't changed."

I couldn't look at him. If he knew how much I missed his company, he'd beat it off my rock in double time. I pulled the hood back from my sweatshirt. "No stopping change," I said.

We sat quietly for a while. A wind had come up off the water that tossed my hair around my face and felt cool on my skin. Somewhere off to my right, a dog howled and a second dog answered. The waves crashed louder on the beach. It was okay that Tyler and I weren't talking. It felt easy for the moment sitting there next to him, listening to the night sounds.

"Do you ever wonder if it's worth it sometimes?" Tyler asked.

I turned to look at his face in profile. In the shadowy light, he was staring straight ahead as if he couldn't take his eyes off whatever it was he was watching that hovered beyond us in the dark. He shifted his leg away from mine. His hair was blowing back from his face and he looked younger than sixteen.

"What is it, Tyler?" My voice was almost a whisper. I put my hand next to his on the rock. I wanted to touch him, but didn't feel that I could.

"I just can't see an end to all the crap some days. It drags me down, you know?"

Something in his voice made me sad. "It'll get better," I said. "We all know these are the hard years. At least, that's what my mom says."

"Your mom. She's a good person. You're lucky to have a mom like her. She's a lot more fun to be around than mine, that's for damn sure." He turned to me and laughed. He picked up my hand and squeezed it before letting it go. "Sorry for getting all weird there. You're just so easy to talk to."

I tried to get over the fact that he'd just grabbed my hand. I took a breath. "Is something going on with you?" I asked. "Something you want to talk about?"

"Life's good. I was just ... getting sidetracked. Mom wants to put Andrew into a group home but Dad says no. She says raising a mentally handicapped son has worn her out, but Dad doesn't want any son of his living with other freaks. His words, not mine."

"What does Andrew want to do? He's eighteen now, right?"

"Yeah, he's eighteen. He wants to leave and have a girlfriend and do all the things normal people do, but he's not normal. Never has been and never will be."

"Where is he now? I haven't seen him around."

"Dad finally agreed to let him stay in the group home until September. Now my parents are fighting over whether he should come home or not." Tyler shrugged and stopped talking. After a bit, he said, "It's nice sometimes though to think of you sitting here on this rock, watching the waves and writing in your book. I've missed being friends. I know what I did to hurt you, and I'm sorry."

"It's okay." I took a breath. "I missed you too."

"I guess we're friends then." I could see his lips curve into a smile. "So how's your old man these days?"

"Not great. He's getting more and more obsessive about stuff, and flies off the handle for nothing."

Tyler sat still for a few seconds then turned toward me. "Do you ever wonder what he'd be like if your sister hadn't died?"

"All the time." I closed my eyes for a second and pushed my face into the wind. It felt good on my skin. "Dad hates coming up here. He wanted Mom to sell the store, but she wouldn't because it was her dad's and she spent every summer here when she was little. After Annie died, Dad couldn't handle this place. Even after all this time, he just comes weekends and leaves early Sunday. He's never been back to Minnow Beach."

"I'm sorry, Dar. I shouldn't have brought it up."

"It was so long ago, I don't think about it much. Ten years is a long time. I was just six when she drowned." I didn't talk about the dull ache in my chest when I thought of Annie or the weird dreams I had sometimes that she was still alive. "Since my dad got sick, we all act like the accident didn't happen, like there never was an Annie. But I used to hear Mom crying in her room when I came home from school for a long time after she died. When Mom heard me in the house, she'd come out of her bedroom and pretend like nothing was wrong. She put away all the pictures of Annie so we wouldn't be reminded."

"If you ever need to talk ... "

"I know."

We sat for a while longer not saying anything, then Tyler stood and stretched his arms into the sky. "It's too dark for you to write any more. You ready to go? I'll walk you home."

"Yeah, I'm ready."

Tyler left me at the footpath to our house. I listened to his footsteps smack the road as he jogged away from me until they were only a faint echo in the distance. Then I slowly started up the path to our store.

Monday morning, I'd picked up another babysitting job not far from Gideon's. After I'd earned my two-fifty, I biked over to see him. He didn't answer his door and I wandered around into the backyard to find him sitting on the bench next to a bed of yellow daylilies with his head thrown back, snoring. Ruby lay at his feet, her head resting on her front paws. She looked up at me and her tail thump-thumped on the bench leg as I approached, but she didn't get up to meet me as she usually did. I eased myself next to Gideon and gave Ruby's head and ears a good rub. Gideon stirred beside me and his eyes opened.

"Hey, Gideon. You looked peaceful sleeping in the sun."

"Little Fin. I was just saying to Ruby that you'd probably be by today."

Gideon's voice was full of phlegm and he turned his head to cough. He leaned forward and spat on the ground.

"You should see a doctor about that cough," I said. "You might have bronchitis or even pneumonia." I'd had pneumonia twice and had been really sick the second time when I was twelve. I'd had to spend three weeks in the hospital, and soon after that they'd removed my tonsils. Gideon's cough sounded worse than mine, and there had been times I'd thought I was coughing up a lung.

"I've seen a doctor and he has me on some medicine. It's probably what's making me sleep in the middle of the day. Nothing to worry about. Let's head inside for some tea. You can make it if you're wanting to look after me."

He smiled his quick smile and we stood together. Nanny was bleating in her pen on the other side of the yard.

"Silly old goat," Gideon said. "Thinks she's a real person. Probably heard our voices and figured she should be in on the excitement. I'll see to her while you go make the tea. I might need to give her a bit more lunch."

"Okay."

I stopped at the back door and turned to look at Gideon. He was moving stiffly and more hunched over than normal. I watched him open the shed door and step inside before I opened the screen door to enter his kitchen.

We sat in our usual chairs, Gideon in his desk chair and me in his leather recliner. We sipped our tea and I felt myself relaxing. Gideon set his cup next to him on the desktop ringed in coffee stains and scarred by cigarette burns. He said, "Have a little project for you, if you're interested. I'll pay since I know it'll take away from the store and babysitting."

"A project?"

"Yeah. A writing project. I'd like you to do the legwork on an article I promised to one of those fancy ladies' magazines. I meant to do it myself but between writing my column in the *Globe* and a few poems and articles I got on the go, this particular project won't get the attention it needs."

"What's this article about?"

"It's about life in cottage land. The pros. The cons. What it means to those who own a cottage and come back year after year. What it's like for new cottagers."

"I could collect information about that," I said excitedly. Already a storyline was taking shape in my head. "I could interview some people and get their quotes and bring you enough to write an excellent piece."

"Exactly what the magazine is after. If you could take a few photos too, that should be enough. I can lend you my camera over on the shelf there."

I glanced at him to see if he was kidding. Gideon's Canon 35mm camera was his baby. He developed his own photos in a darkroom he'd set up in one of the bedrooms. I'd worked with him often, developing black and white pictures as he taught me the process, hanging the pictures by clothes pegs on a line he'd strung over the workbench.

"How long will the article be?"

"Oh, a few thousand words. Maybe three thousand. The important thing is to tell an interesting story and to add some human interest."

"I'll get you some good information. You can count on it, Gideon."

"Good girl. Why don't you go get the camera and I'll show you how to use it properly. I also have a notepad you can take as my official sidekick in training."

I saluted and grinned. "Darlene Findley, a.k.a. Little Fin, at your service."

Gideon grunted and his smile came and went. "Pull up a chair and after I talk about the finer points of this camera, we'll go over the steps to writing a good article. You have lots to learn if I'm going to make a journalist out of you."

I couldn't meet Gideon's eyes. I would never be a journalist. It wasn't in my future no matter how much I wanted it. My dad would never stand for me having a career that would take me that far from home. He'd already told me not to plan on going to university like William. Secretaries didn't need a higher education.

Elizabeth and I sat on the front steps of the store after supper a few days later. She'd tuned her little pocket radio to CHUM FM in Toronto and we were listening to Casey Kasem's top forty of the week. It was a hot evening and we decided to put up with the blackflies and mosquitoes instead of being shut up indoors where the air was stifling. At least on the front steps, there was a whisper of a breeze. Elizabeth fanned herself with a page from the newspaper that she'd taken from the store.

"In Toronto, we have air conditioning," she said, "and no damn blackflies."

"Can't you go back if you want to?"

"My parents said if I lasted here, they'd buy me a car in the fall. I've already picked it out — a shiny silver Mustang." She laughed. "My father promised it'll be sitting in the driveway Labour Day weekend on condition I don't arrive home before then."

"They must really hate Michael if they're willing to bribe you with a car so you stay away from him."

"Well, they sent me to live with your dad, so what does that tell you?"

The meanness of her words cut. "My dad's not so bad."

"He's low class, Dar. He can't keep a decent job and he … well, he doesn't even read books."

"He may not have had all the chances your dad had, but my dad's not low class. He works hard for our family. Why do you pretend you like him when he's around if you think he's so bad?"

Elizabeth laughed, like she was humouring me. "I'm sorry for what I said. I didn't mean low class. I just meant he has rigid ideas and he's got to have everything just so or he goes crazy, that's all. You're so quick to take things the wrong way."

"Maybe he has to have things organized all the time, but that's not a crime." I couldn't let it go. "My dad thinks you like him."

Elizabeth put the newspaper she'd been waving back and forth onto the step next to her. "Lots of people think I like them. That's not a crime either."

"Like Michael?"

"Yeah, like him."

"I don't want you to talk about my dad any more. I don't want you saying anything to me or to my friends about my family."

Elizabeth held up her hands, pretending to surrender. "I won't say anything bad about your dad ever again. Promise. Cross my heart and hope to die. Sheesh. Who knew you were so sensitive?"

"I wouldn't call me sensitive. I call what you said insensitive."

"Yeah, it probably was." She bumped me gently with her hip. "Most people wouldn't have cared. It's not everyone who would defend their crazy father." She laughed and held up her hands again. "Just kidding, I swear."

"Quit while you're ahead," I said. "Or I might have to deck you one." I said it tough, but we both knew I wouldn't.

"God knows I'd deserve it."

I was quiet for a bit. "Will you keep dating Michael when you're back home?"

Elizabeth smiled and shrugged. "His letters were starting to bore me, you know, wanting me to be his all his, he couldn't live without me ... so I wrote him and told him it was over. Now, he writes that he wants to come to Cedar Lake to see me this week."

"What will you tell him?"

"Not to bother. It's over."

She looked at me with probing grey eyes. Her voice got solemn. "And I know your dad was responsible for Annie drowning, and he had a breakdown that took a few years coming and he's never been right since."

"I don't want to talk about it."

"Nobody does. Maybe that's the big fat problem. The whole damn family pretends like nothing ever happened."

I heard a noise behind me and looked up at the same time as Elizabeth.

"Do you need something, Mom?" I asked. I could feel my heart thudding inside my chest. How long had she been standing there?

Her eyes darted between me and Elizabeth. "I thought I might go for a walk. Do you girls think you could watch the store for an hour or so?"

I tried to read my mom's face through the black mesh of the screen. She didn't look like she'd heard what we'd been talking about and I relaxed a bit. I glanced at Elizabeth. I could tell she was watching too and sizing up our words and body language. I needed to keep her from reading something into my mother's outing. I wondered where she'd be meeting up with Johnny.

"No problem, Mom."

"Yes, Aunt Jan. Darlene and I can watch the store for you."

Mom pushed the screen door open and stepped outside. She was wearing a purple tank top and white denim shorts. She'd pulled her hair back into a ponytail and looked closer to twenty than forty. She wiped a hand across the beads of sweat on her forehead and said, "I just need a break. You girls can have an ice cream if you like. Whew, it sure is hot."

Elizabeth and I watched Mom go down the path, walking through the ribbons of shadow until she disappeared behind the thicket of evergreen trees that led to the lake. Elizabeth reached down and turned off her radio. She picked it up and pushed herself to her feet.

"I need to go upstairs and get something," she said. "I'll be right back."

After she'd been gone ten minutes and I knew she wouldn't be returning, I went inside the store and took out the notebook Gideon had given me from its hiding place under the counter. I didn't want Elizabeth to know I was working on this project, so I was keeping the notebook in a place she'd never look. I'd jotted down some notes and ideas on two pages as well as possible people to interview. I'd also started writing an opening for the story. I knew Gideon would be writing the version for the magazine, but I wanted to try my hand at a finished story too. I was ready to begin interviewing my first candidate. Tomorrow would be my first official day as a magazine writer. I could hardly wait to get started. It gave me something to hold on to.

Chapter Eight

I ROLLED OVER AND opened my eyes. The sun was streaming through the open curtains onto the floor and the hands of the clock read six thirty. I closed my eyes and tried to go back to sleep, but it was no use — too many things on my mind. I wanted to get started on my writing assignment and William and Dad should be at the lake early in the afternoon. I had a lot to do before they showed up and Dad started finding chores for me around the house.

I slipped out from under the covers and stretched. By the stifling air in the bedroom, I could tell it was going to be another hot day. Elizabeth didn't stir as I slid open my dresser drawer and took out my favourite denim shorts and white cotton peasant top. I took them into the bathroom and changed, then washed my face, brushed my teeth, and went downstairs. Mom wasn't up yet, so I tried to move around quietly as I searched the cupboards for something to eat. A package of unopened bran muffins was at the back of the bread cupboard. I checked for green mold then ate one with a glass of orange juice before collecting my notebook and pen and heading out the back door.

The heat hit me like a wall when I stepped outside, even though the sun was barely up above the pine trees. Sweat was running down my forehead and cheeks by the time I'd left our backyard and started down the path to the road. My shirt was sticky against my skin, as if someone had dribbled warm water down my back. I looked up and down the empty road and started walking in the direction of Tyler's house. He might not want to help me with my article for Gideon, but I hoped he would. He was the perfect person to talk about growing up at the lake and what it meant now we were older.

I didn't meet him on the way as I'd hoped I would. I started walking slower. I rounded the bend and spotted his cottage, which was set in a stand of alders on a bluff a fair distance from the water. As I got closer, I started to rethink my plan. Maybe it wasn't such a good idea after all. Tyler might think I was chasing him and I'd look pathetic. I hesitated at the bottom of his driveway. I began turning to retrace my steps when the back door of the cottage opened. Tyler had chosen that exact moment to come outside holding a big orange tabby cat. He set it down on the steps and gave the back of its neck a scratch before he raised his head to survey the yard. That's when he saw me. There was nowhere to hide. I waved and started up the driveway as if I was happy to see him.

"You're up early," he said. "Give me a sec and I'll walk with you."

He went back inside, giving me time to think about what I would say. A few minutes later, he opened the back door and leapt down the stairs, carrying his lunch pail and drinking from a bottle of orange juice. His hair was damp and beads of sweat glistened on his forehead.

"Too hot to run today," he said. "I have time to sit by the lake for a bit till my ride comes, if you want to."

We walked back toward my cottage and the path to the beach.

"Were you looking for me?" he asked.

"Maybe."

"Just like old times." He grinned and bumped me with his lunch pail. "Remember the time I dared you to climb that huge pine tree on Old Bear Road and the wind came up and you were swaying up there holding on for dear life?"

"As I recall, you didn't tell me the tree leaked sap. It took me two days to get my hands clean. I had some explaining to do when I got home and my clothes were ruined. That scared me more than falling out of the tree."

Tyler laughed. "I sure liked watching you climb. You were like a squirrel hopping up those branches. You could outclimb all the guys."

"With my hands tied," I said. "But I've outgrown climbing trees."

In case you hadn't noticed.

We walked silently down the path through the trees and across the sand until we reached my rock overlooking the water. This morning the lake was velvety blue and still as glass. Tyler leaned back and stretched his legs while he drank his orange juice. He sighed like he was happy to be sitting on my rock, and I pretended for a few seconds that I was the reason.

"I'm helping Gideon with a story he's working on for a magazine and wonder if I could get your opinion on summers at the lake," I said.

"Gideon, that old man who delivers the mail?"

"He's actually a journalist. He has a column in a Toronto paper."

"Really? I thought he was a retired guy from Toronto who just enjoys living like a hermit."

"Yeah well, looks can be deceiving. So, will you do it? Answer a few questions for my article?"

Tyler lowered the bottle. "Okay, I guess. Sure, ask away."

"Great."

I opened my notebook to a clean page and uncapped my pen. "So what do you remember about summers at the lake when you were young?"

Tyler looked out over the lake and squinted into the sun. "I remember I could hardly wait to leave Peterborough to come here when school got out. There always seemed to be lots of kids around and no end of things to do — swimming, touring around in the rowboat, camping under the stars, bonfires. It was a free time. No worries except remembering to show up home for supper. There was a certain girl I used to like to hang out with." He turned sideways and grinned at me. "Seems I still do."

I ducked my head so he wouldn't see my face change colour. I'd forgotten how much he liked to tease me.

"How has it changed, coming up to the lake?"

This time, Tyler was quiet for a long time. When he started talking, his voice had lost its lightness. "It's like all the fun has gone out of being here. I don't know when it changed, but it did. I'd rather be in Toronto or Ottawa or anywhere else where there's something going on. It's like I'm just putting in time. Waiting for my life to begin and doing everything possible not to end up working a nine to five job like my dad."

"Would you really rather be in the city?"

"Sometimes. Maybe not." Tyler focused his eyes on the horizon. "I thought about signing up for Nam over the winter. I wanted to get out there and see the world and do something different. Get away for a while."

My heart jumped. "It's not our war. It's the Americans' war."

"They take Canadian recruits. We're still part of it whether we want to be or not. Anyhow, I decided I couldn't stand killing anyone, so that ended that daydream."

"Being shot at wouldn't be much fun either."

"I ask myself why I should lead this safe life while people are being killed." Tyler's voice had dropped.

"We can't be responsible for the terrible things going on in the world," I said. "You aren't the one who decided to send troops into Vietnam."

"But I'm watching from the sidelines. Who said that evil is sitting back doing nothing while people are dying?"

"Edmund Burke in the 1700s. He said that all it takes for evil to triumph is good men to do nothing."

Tyler shot me an admiring look. "How do you know this stuff?"

"History class. It's a pretty famous quote."

"Yeah, but how many people remember who said it? Anyhow, that's what we're doing, in my opinion."

"But how could you want to fight in a war after what happened to those women and children in My Lai? How many was it the Americans slaughtered? Five hundred? They herded them up like animals and shot them. Look at the Kent State massacre last year. The Ohio National Guard fired on students. They killed four of them and wounded nine more just because they were protesting going into Cambodia. They weren't much older than you or me. How can they rationalize doing that? It's wrong what Nixon's doing. What their government is making their soldiers do. The Americans aren't blameless." I was out of breath.

"Yeah, but sometimes you have to take a stand even if it doesn't all go perfectly."

"I don't know if we do in Vietnam," I said. "How can we know what's really behind a country going to war when politicians will say anything to get what they want?"

"You've got me there. I just think there's more reason to go to Vietnam than not. I guess we can agree to disagree." Tyler looked at his watch. "Hey, gotta go. My ride will be here soon." He stood and looked down at me. "You coming to the beach party tonight? You can ask me more questions, then, for your lake article if you want. We seem to have a lot to talk about." He grinned.

"I'm not sure. William will be visiting for the weekend." The sudden change in topic left me wanting to hear more of Tyler's opinions about Vietnam. Tyler was smarter than he let on most of the time. We used to discuss things going on in the world before he found Jane Ratherford and turned cool.

"Bring him too. I haven't seen your brother all year."

"Maybe."

"See you then."

I watched Tyler walk across the beach before I returned to my notebook. He hadn't told me much that I could use in my article, but a new idea was beginning to take shape. This could be a coming of age story — the childhood security of Cedar Lake and the war raging across the ocean. I knew Canada wasn't officially in the war, but we were too closely connected to the States to believe that it wasn't our war too. Gideon had said that enough times to make me a believer. This could be the angle that would transform my story into something brilliant.

I jotted down notes for well over an hour. When I finally put away my pen, I was ready to interview more people. I thought again about Tyler and wondered if it meant anything that he hadn't asked about Elizabeth. I ran that idea around in my mind like a warm beach stone, trying to read something into his omission, but in the end, I couldn't convince myself that what he'd failed to ask meant anything at all.

~••~

I waited another hour before going to Candy Parsens'. I'd picked her as my token newcomer at the lake, figuring she'd give my article an exotic flavour. If I was lucky, she'd name more of her famous friends.

I pedalled my bike up their driveway and surveyed their property. The grass hadn't been mowed in a while and the shrubs that used to be trimmed obsessively by Mr. Davidson were starting to grow in haphazard shapes. Bags of garbage were stacked near the back door and empty wine bottles spilled out of one. Flies circled just above and wasps buzzed from the pile. The visitor's car was still in the driveway behind Johnny's flower power van.

I got halfway up the driveway before I stopped and thought about leaving and coming back another time. I didn't want to walk in on Candy and Johnny and those two men staying with them. Another few seconds and I would have been gone, but just like at Tyler's, the back door opened before I'd taken a step away from the house. Candy must have seen me through the kitchen window. She started running toward me. Her flowing caftan, the colour of rubies, was shimmering in the sunlight with each step. As she got closer, I could see that the scooped neckline was rimmed in gold and silver threads. Under the hem of the caftan, her toenails were painted bubble gum pink. Candy waved a cigarette in the air as she reached around me with her other arm to give me a hug. She reeked of nicotine and Tabu, the heaviest drugstore perfume going.

"Darlene, did we make plans for today? I was hoping

you'd come by. We can go down to the beach for a swim. Johnny's looking after the baby."

I stared at her. Hadn't she remembered begging me to come visit?

She took me by the hand and tugged me toward the cottage, giggling as if we were two teenage girlfriends. I let myself be propelled along until I found myself in the kitchen. Johnny looked up from where he was spooning food into Sean's open mouth. Sean was seated in a high chair, banging a lettered block on the plastic tray in between mouthfuls. The kitchen was even messier than the last time I'd been in it, with boxes of food and food-encrusted dishes spread about the surfaces along with overflowing ashtrays. If I lived to be ninety, I'd never be able to stomach the smell of rotting food. Johnny looked down at the bowl of oatmeal he was holding as Candy spoke to him.

"We're going to the beach for a bit. You'll be okay here?"

"I thought you were going to clean up the place today."

Candy shrugged. "It'll still be here in an hour. Surely you can live with the way things are until then."

"Do I have a choice?"

"We always have a choice," said Candy. She spun around to face me. "Wait here and I'll just go get my bag and stuff."

She crossed the kitchen and disappeared down the hallway, leaving me alone with Johnny and Sean. I felt awkward standing in the entranceway. I couldn't think of anything to say. Johnny kept feeding Sean as if I wasn't there. I cleared my throat.

"Those two guys are still visiting," I said. "Bobby and Kirk." Their names had popped into my head. Not that it was any of my business, but it was the only conversation opener I could come up with.

Johnny straightened up in the chair. He stopped the spoonful of oatmeal in mid-air. "I didn't realize you'd met them." He turned to look at me. Every time I saw his black eyes, they made me lose my train of thought. He waited while I got my mouth to work.

"I just ran into them the other afternoon. They were in the backyard with Candy and Sean."

"Ahh." Johnny turned back around and attempted to put the spoon into Sean's mouth. Sean held his lips tightly closed and shook his head back and forth, all the while banging the block on the tray. Oatmeal flew from the spoon when the block smacked Johnny's hand. "Had enough then, little man?" Johnny picked up the bottom of Sean's bib and wiped away the oatmeal clinging to his face with gentle strokes. "Time to play then." He looked at me. "They're leaving soon. Bobby and Kirk. Just friends passing through." He waited again for me to say something.

"Oh." I said. *Could I get any more brilliant?* "Did you know them when you lived in the States?"

"We met Johnny a few years ago when we were involved in the same business venture, isn't that right, old friend?" I turned. Bobby had walked into the kitchen and joined into the conversation. A cigarette hung out of his mouth and bobbed up and down as he talked. He grabbed a chair on the other side of the table and straddled it so his arms were folded on the back. His afro surrounded his head like a beach ball.

Johnny glanced over. "Where's Kirk?"

"Sleeping. We drained a twenty-sixer of Jim Beam last night. Feeling a little rough myself." He scratched his chest. "Bummer."

Johnny looked at me. "Maybe you'd rather wait outside. Candy won't be long."

I had my hand on the doorknob as Candy came back into the kitchen. She was swinging a straw handbag and had put on green granny sunglasses. She'd loosened her hair from the knot at the back of her head, and it hung long and thick on her shoulders.

"All set," she said.

"Loooking goooood, Mama," said Bobby. He let out a low whistle."

"Watch yourself," said Johnny. His mouth was smiling, but his eyes weren't.

"Why, jealous?" asked Candy. She stepped closer to the table and ran a hand through Bobby's afro. "Bobby here's just being sociable, isn't that right, sugar?"

"Chill, man," said Bobby. "Just showing my appreciation to the little hostess."

Johnny lowered Sean onto the floor. Candy barely glanced at them. She ignored Sean reaching up toward her, his arms wide and his mouth working like a fish.

"All set. We'll be back soon," Candy said as she opened the back door. "Try not to miss me."

"We'll give it our best shot," said Johnny as the door closed behind us.

"Hurry back," called Bobby loud enough so we could hear him through the open window "You know I'll be here waiting."

Candy and I didn't talk as we climbed down the path toward the lake. I could tell she was still angry about whatever was going on between her and Johnny. When we reached the beach, she immediately pulled her red caftan over her head. Underneath was a white bikini. She pulled up a strap that had fallen in a loop down her arm before she started running toward the lake. The water was satin blue, reflecting the colour of the sky.

"Coming in?" she called over her shoulder.

"Maybe later. I'm working on something."

I wanted to keep writing while ideas were fresh. I didn't feel much like swimming with her anyhow. If it wasn't for the article, I would have gone home.

She spent twenty minutes furiously swimming around the bay before coming over to flop down next to me in the sand. A shower of lake water splashed on my legs and book cover. I wiped the book quickly on my shorts, upset that splotches would stain the leather cover. Candy lay flat on her back, not caring about the sand that would work into her hair and cake onto her skin.

"Johnny's such an ass sometimes," she said, but she was smiling again. She propped herself up on her elbows so that she was looking at the water. "Why did you come by this morning anyhow?"

"Well, we did make plans…." My voice trailed away.

It didn't seem like a good idea to remind her about what she'd forgotten and the money she owed me. "Anyhow, I'm helping Gideon write a story for a magazine about life in Cedar Lake. I wondered if I could interview you as a newcomer to the lake."

"An interview? Why, that sounds like fun. You are such a little sugar pie to think of me for your story."

"You've led an interesting life," I said. It was nice to see her happy again.

"Oh, I could tell you some stories! Why, I was at the Pentagon anti-war demonstration in '67, putting flowers in the guns of the National Guard. I'm in one of the photos *Life* magazine printed, not the cover, but still, I was part of history. Flower power. That was a trip. Yeah, I could be in your article as long as you don't use my real name." She sat up and wrapped one arm around her legs, pulling her hair away from her face with her other hand. She shifted slightly and stared at me, her eyes wide and unblinking.

"What was it like being there?" I asked. "In D.C.?"

"Oh man. We were about fifty thousand marching across the Memorial Bridge and the troops were all lined up to greet us on the Pentagon steps, like a human barricade to keep us out. We were singing the whole time, trying to drive away the evil spirits. Some tried to get in one of the entrances and the guards threw them down the steps. I stayed the night and got arrested in the morning for picking flowers in Lafayette Park. It was a rush, I can tell you. We were taking on the establishment, making them take notice."

"I would have given anything to be there too."

"Yeah, it was worth the trip, but you would have been what, ten years old?"

"Twelve.

"I was at Woodstock too, with Janis. Three days of peace and love and rock and roll. August '69. We landed in the field in a helicopter but Janis wasn't cool with the set-up. They had her playing at two in the morning. Still, she gave a bitchin' show. What I'd give to go back to those days." She looked at me. "Johnny doesn't want me talking about this stuff anymore. He says we're starting fresh in Canada and Sean shouldn't be contaminated by what's going on in the States, especially the war."

"In my article, I could call you Cindy Peters," I said.

"Cindy Peters. Cool. I like that."

"Okay then ..." I opened my book to a clean page and uncapped my pen. "To start with, why did you choose to spend a summer in Cedar Lake?"

"Johnny chose it. He had good memories of being here as a kid. Said it was a happy retreat from life in the States. He wanted a break from the city and thought Sean could do with a summer in the country, and you know ... to get away from the war."

"So life was hectic and you needed a break?"

"Something like that."

Candy started rifling through her bag.

"How did the Vietnam War impact your life in the States?"

Candy's hand, still deep in the bag, stopped moving. She turned her face toward me. "What makes you ask that?"

"It's just an angle I'm going with. You know, the peace of Cedar Lake in contrast to what's going on internationally."

She looked back into her bag and pulled out a cigarette and then a lighter. She lit the cigarette with an unsteady hand before she looked at me and said, "Look, you seem like a nice kid. Can we talk off the record?"

"I guess."

I closed my book but kept my hand inserted to mark my spot. Gideon would have said there is no off the record, but it wouldn't feel right if I used something she didn't want me to make public. I waited while Candy inhaled and held the smoke in her lungs. It shot from her nose in two long white streams.

"Johnny was there. Vietnam. It's not something he likes to talk about."

"Did you know him before he went overseas?"

"Johnny was dating my sister. They were supposed to get married."

"What happened?"

"Frances … my sister, met someone else while he was stationed in Nam. She thought she'd just have this fling until Johnny came back. Hell, she had this fear, pardon me, a damn *premonition* he was going to be killed over there. She told me often enough anyway. Kind of ironic, in hindsight. He was a fighter pilot and flew over some of the worst areas dropping bombs. Anyhow, Johnny being in danger's way gave Frances a reason to fool around, at least in her own mind. I know it's unkind to speak ill of the dead, but Frances wasn't the kind of girl who could be alone for long."

"So how did you ..."

"End up with Johnny?" Candy took a puff of her cigarette and laughed as she exhaled. "Sean is his son, as you may have guessed, but Frances is the mother. Johnny and I aren't married. I know you thought we were married, and I kind of liked letting you think that." She smiled. "Anyhow, Johnny and Frances hooked up briefly after he came back from Nam, before he found out she was seeing someone else. Johnny took off when he found out. When Frances died, I followed him to Canada with the baby. It looks too much like him not to be his."

"Then you're not ... ?"

"Together? A couple?" Her voice was bitter. "Sometimes yes. Sometimes no. It all depends on Johnny's mood on a particular day. I can assure you, that he isn't the man he was before he went to Nam. Something is missing, you know, like he's been damaged beyond repair."

I thought of my mom. She'd met him in the restaurant and he'd come looking for her in the store. Worry spread through my veins like water seeping into cracks. "Why don't you leave?"

"I keep hoping he'll come to his senses, take a look around and realize I'm the girl for him now that Frances is gone." Candy started digging in the sand with the toes of one foot. She looked at me and smiled, her lips pulled sideways. "I know it must seem like I'm out of my mind to you. I loved him even when he was with Frances, which I know you think is probably just plain awful, but you can't control who you fall for. I wish you could, but love doesn't work that way. Frances was weak and not good enough for him. The better woman is alive and waiting." She laughed but her eyes were sad. "Maybe I'll take off soon. Maybe I'll find love with someone else. Who knows? It's not like I haven't had offers. A few of them were even kind of nice."

"I guess it would be hard for you to leave Sean behind."

"In some ways, yeah, but it would be wonderful not to be responsible for anyone again. I'm not really wired that way, if you haven't noticed. If it weren't for Johnny …" Candy stopped talking and took a long drag of her cigarette before flicking it into the sand where it lay a glowing ember. She watched it for a bit and then lifted her eyes toward the lake. "Thing is. Some things he doesn't forgive too easily."

I opened my notebook again and said, "Maybe, I could ask you my questions now, you know, for the interview."

Candy swiped with the back of her hand at a tear that had trickled halfway down her cheek. She laughed self-consciously before saying, "Fire away. I think it'll be a kick to be quoted in a magazine like I have something worth sharing with the world. Something for the grand-kids to see."

"I hope the article turns out okay. It's my first attempt at this kind of writing."

"I have the utmost confidence. Just don't write anything bad about me and don't mention Johnny or

Vietnam. He hates newspapers and magazines more than anything. He really is fanatical about our privacy because of Sean."

"I won't mention either one of them."

"That's good. This'll just be between you and me, sugar. Our little secret."

I remembered Gideon's camera in my bag. "Maybe I could take a picture of you looking at the lake. I could just do a shot from the side so nobody sees your whole face."

Candy laughed. "You're one smart kid, you know that? I guess it would be okay. There have to be lots of blonde girls in this world who look just like me if you don't look too closely."

Chapter Nine

MY PARENTS WERE talking with William in the kitchen. I'd entered the store and could see my mother as she moved back and forth from counter to table, setting out the meal she'd prepared especially for my brother's homecoming. Pork roast, scalloped potatoes, broccoli with cheese sauce, and apple pie with Velveeta cheese for dessert. The talking stopped as I walked across the floor to stand in the doorway. William looked up at me and grinned. Elizabeth was sitting in the seat next to him, looking pretty in an aqua sleeveless blouse, her hair tied back with a silky white scarf. Her elbows rested on the table, one hand tucked under her chin while the other twirled a gold locket around and around.

"Come sit here," said William, patting the empty chair on his other side. "Your ears must be ringing because we were just talking about you."

"Uh-oh," I said. "Anything you can repeat?"

William laughed. "All good. I was just catching up on what you've been doing. You're looking well."

"You too." I slid in next to him and he reached over and ruffled my hair.

"I think you're a few inches taller that last time I saw you."

"It happens," I said.

I looked him over. His hair had reached his shoulders and he'd grown a beard. The sleeves of his white shirt were rolled up and he wore a leather strip around one wrist. By the way Elizabeth was watching him, I knew she didn't care that they were cousins. I'd gotten used to the way girls looked at my brother, and it didn't make me uncomfortable like it used to.

My dad's eyes settled on mine. "Where've you been all afternoon?"

"Just at the beach and then I stopped by Candy Parsens' .... "

His eyes narrowed. "I don't like you spending time there," he said. "There's something not right about that family."

My mother was standing by the counter. She turned and her eyes darted to my father. She was upset.

"How do you know what they're like?" I asked. I knew immediately I'd made a big mistake.

The vein in my dad's temple throbbed purple. He stared me down until I felt my bottom lip quiver. He threw his fork onto his plate and it made a loud clink that made my knee jump and bang against the bottom of the table. "It doesn't take but one sighting to know they're trouble. Long-haired, hippy, weirdo freaks." He punctuated each word like he was punching holes in a piece of paper. He looked across the table at William to let my brother know what he thought of his appearance too. "I'm sick of these freeloaders moving in and taking over the neighborhood. The woman dresses like a prostitute. The man probably pushes drugs to kids in playgrounds. I'd like to line them up and ..."

"That's enough, George," my mother said quietly. "We get the point."

My father looked at my mother. "How do we know they aren't up to no good? We can't just turn a blind eye and pretend everybody's welcome in the community. Some bring drugs and immoral behaviour. We have to be on guard."

Next to me, William tensed, and I felt him move his feet back from where they'd been stretched out under the table. I kept my eyes on my mother's face. She was watching my dad.

"Not everyone is a threat, George."

"I know that, but you can tell a lot about someone by how they dress. I have a bad feeling about that family."

"You have a bad feeling about everyone."

She spoke so softly that if we hadn't been holding our collective breath, I might have missed what she'd said. She turned her back on my father and continued calmly chopping the tomato she'd be adding to the salad bowl on the counter. Her back was ramrod straight, her shoulders squared.

My father looked at her without moving for a few seconds. Then he stood up and raised a hand as if he was dismissing the whole lot of us. His voice wasn't as angry as it had been, though. "I'll just go move those boxes for you then, before suppertime."

"That would be good," my mother said without turning.

Dad glared at me before he clumped from the room as if I was responsible for getting him into trouble. The front door banged shut behind him.

William stood too. "Need anything, Mom?" he asked.

She laid the knife carefully on the counter. "I think I'll go check on the laundry if you could finish this salad, Darlene." She turned and smiled at us without really focusing. I nodded and watched her leave the kitchen.

William sat back down. He slumped hard against the chair.

"What was that all about?" Elizabeth asked. "Is your father always so … paranoid about people? You'd think Charles Manson had moved his commune in next door the way he acts."

"He has his moments," I said. I wouldn't give her room to ask anything else. I wouldn't let her see how shaken I was by my father's anger. I swung around to face my brother. "How's school going, William?"

"Good. Good." He looked at me. "It's harder this year, but I'm enjoying the challenge. Tell me about grade ten. Did you ace it?"

His eyes flashed a warning at me. I knew to pretend like nothing had happened.

"Not so much, but I passed okay."

"You must be the smart side of the family tree," said Elizabeth. Her blonde hair trailed on the table as she leaned forward toward my brother. "Will you defend me when you get to be a big time lawyer?"

"You plan to do something illegal."

"Everything I plan to do is illegal." She smiled at William.

"Maybe Dad should start looking for trouble a little closer to home," I said, "instead of worrying about the hippies down the road."

After dinner, I looked for William all over the house and in the backyard. I needed to talk to him. I went back to the living room. Elizabeth raised her head from where she was lying on the couch watching *Laugh-In*. Ruth Buzzy was hitting an old man over the head with her purse. I looked at Elizabeth and had the urge to grab something and thwack her too. It was the second time I'd gone into the back room looking for my brother. Elizabeth hadn't answered when I asked her the first time if knew where he was. This time, she kept her eyes on the screen when I entered and she let out a loud sigh.

"He's gone out. He said he'd be back in time to go to the beach with us."

"Why didn't you say that last time I asked? It would have saved me looking all over for him."

Elizabeth tossed her hair back and stared me down from her prone position. "I knew you'd figure it out. You're a smart girl."

"And you're a …"

"Darlene," my mother was right behind me, "could you watch the store for a minute?"

I turned. Her eyes were fixed on me, and I couldn't do anything but nod.

"See you later," said Elizabeth. "Do you want to watch TV with me, Aunt Jan?"

"No thanks, Elizabeth. I have an errand to run and then I'll be back in the store."

"Where are you going?" I asked.

"Just out for some fresh air." Mom laughed. "Not really an errand I guess."

I started down the road toward Candy's cottage after Mom came back from her walk and took over the cash. Anywhere would be better than staying home and spending time with Elizabeth. I knew I shouldn't react when she baited me, but knowing and stopping myself were two different things.

The night air was warm with a full moon and a blanket of stars punched out like sequins overhead. It felt good walking through the darkness and listening to the crickets in the long grass. I thought about climbing down the path to my rock to watch the water but kept walking along the road. I was getting closer to Candy's cottage and heard voices up ahead. Men's voices. I slowed down and tried to blend into the shadows closer to the side of the road. The voices stopped and someone was walking toward me. He had his head down and it took me a few seconds to recognize him. I stepped forward, crossing the road to block William's path.

"Darlene," he said. "Where'd you come from?"

"I was looking for you. Who were you just talking to?"

William half turned around, then swung back toward me. "Just met the guy staying in the Davidson cottage for the summer."

"That's Johnny Lewis. Did you run into him on the road?"

"Yeah, I met up with Mom, but she had to go back to the store. I didn't feel ready to go in yet so headed this way and Johnny was out walking. We just got talking."

We started back toward our house. "What did he say?" I asked. "You seemed to be having quite a conversation."

"Talked about the weather mostly. Seems like an okay guy."

"I don't know. Whenever I see him, I get the feeling he's hiding something."

William laughed. "You're one spooky kid some-times, you know that?"

"What do you mean?"

"I forget sometimes how intuitive you are, but we all keep secrets you know. I'll bet you've stored up a few since I saw you last. Johnny's probably no different. So how's Dad been?"

Smooth change of topic, I thought. I let it go. "You know. Dad's Dad."

I nearly tripped on a rock in the road and William reached out a hand to steady me. "He seems more agi-tated than normal," he said.

"Dad was laid off again in the spring but it just lasted a few weeks before they called him back. He asked us not to talk about it. You know how he gets when he can't control things. Plus he's getting headaches again."

"Bad ones like before?"

"Yeah."

"That's not good."

"Tell me about it. Mom says he's worried about me getting in with the wrong crowd."

"You giving him reason?"

"Do you really think he needs one?"

I could hear the smile in William's voice. "Probably not. So how are things with you anyway?"

"I could do without our cousin here. What's going on with her parents anyway?"

"Aunt Peg drinks … a lot. She used to just drink at night, but now she starts as soon as she gets up in the morning.

"No way. How long has she been doing that?"

"A long time. Elizabeth's been left on her own since she started high school. Maybe earlier. Uncle Ed doesn't spend much time at home."

I stopped walking. "So the question is, does Uncle Ed not go home because Aunt Peg drinks or does Aunt Peg drink because Uncle Ed doesn't come home?"

"I'd tell you if I knew."

"I still don't like Elizabeth much. Does that make me mean?"

"Not really. She's got that tough act down. Makes it hard to warm up to her."

"She likes you just fine. In fact, she likes most boys just fine."

"Give her a chance, Dar. She's not so bad."

"Spoken like a true male. Oh yeah, and she keeps bringing up Annie. It's like she's trying to throw her death in my face. She has this way of looking at me like I was to blame. Dad looks at me like that too sometimes."

William stopped. He put an arm around my waist and pulled me closer. He leaned into me and spoke low and fierce into my ear. "You were six, Darlene. It wasn't your fault that Dad was looking after you when Annie drowned. You were just a kid."

"Tell that to Dad," I said. "I'm the one he can hardly bear to be around." I was miserable. Being miserable made me angry. "Sometimes I think he wishes it was me instead of Annie. I'll bet Elizabeth would rather it was me too."

William pulled me tighter and my ribs hurt under the pressure of his arm. "It's not an either or deal. You know we'd all be heartbroken if anything had happened to you."

I nodded into his chest.

"We couldn't bear if anything … anything, happened … to … you."

I nodded again, inhaling the smell of the woods and sweat and sincerity that was my brother. "I know," I whispered, but in the empty hollow where my heart beat, I didn't believe him.

He let go of me and we started walking again. A few steps farther on he grabbed my hand. He swung our hands back and forth. We didn't speak again until the lights of the store came into view.

"So, are you seeing anybody?" I asked. "Mom said you broke up with Gail."

"Gail! Man, she was a long time ago. I've been hanging loose, working on my studies, dating a bit."

"You've always got a girlfriend somewhere. Has someone broken your heart?"

"Just taking a breather from women. How about you? Anybody special?"

I shook my head. "Nobody special."

"It's less painful that way, believe me."

His voice was sad. I wished I could see his face more clearly. "So there is someone."

"There was, but it's over. Just sometimes when I see her." He took me by the arm. "I don't know how you've dragged this out of me, but I'm done talking about women and my damaged heart. Buy you an ice cream cone?"

"You're on," I said. "I always could be bought off with ice cream."

"Whatever works to get your mind off my love life. Race you back. I'll give you to the tree as a head start."

I started running. "Get ready to eat my dust," I called over my shoulder.

Chapter Ten

ELIZABETH AND I walked with William across the sand as the sun cast dark shadows across the lake. The day's heat had settled into a milky haze on the water, but a breeze was making the evening more bearable than the day. William pulled a full case of Blue from a cooler in the back seat of his Volkswagen beetle, and after we took up our position between the bonfire and the shoreline, he popped the tops of three beer bottles with an opener and handed us each a semi-cold one. I took a sip and swished the beer around in my mouth before swallowing.

Michelle and Danny were late and I kept searching for them, my eyes sliding past Elizabeth to scan up the beach. When I finally spotted the two of them coming towards us, they weren't holding hands like they usually did and were walking a little apart. I looked at Elizabeth. She'd turned and was watching them too with a little smile on her face. When they made it to our circle, William and I moved away from each other to give them some space. My brother handed them each a beer. Michelle avoided looking at Elizabeth, who was busy tossing around her hair and smiling at Danny — full-on smiling when she saw that Michelle wasn't looking. After a while, Elizabeth moved around me closer to Danny and reached for his hand. Luckily, Michelle was talking to William and turned away from them.

Nearly everyone at the beach party came up to talk to my brother. He welcomed everyone with a handshake or a hug and included them in our ever-widening circle. Ben Murdoch slung an arm around his neck. They'd been best friends at the lake as long as I could remember.

"Ben! How are you, buddy?" William asked.

"So who's the chick in Toronto? She must be really something to keep you from the lake." Ben said.

"Not a she." William turned and spoke into Ben's ear. I tried to listen, but the music was loud and too many people were talking. Ben kept nodding at whatever William was saying. I heard Ben say, "Right on, man. Whatever you need me to do."

A lot of yelling behind us and we all turned to watch Tyler Livingstone swagger across the beach with his arm draped over Jane Ratherford's shoulder. Her entourage of girlfriends trailed behind them, giggling and talking loudly. By the time they made it to our group, I'd stepped back a few paces to be out of range.

"Hey, man," Tyler said, grabbing William by the hand and pumping it up and down. "Darlene told me you were home. Great to see you, man." He looked past

William like he was searching for someone. Elizabeth stepped forward.

"Hi, Tyler. I was wondering if you'd be by tonight."

Tyler squinted, trying to bring my cousin into focus. Jane grabbed him by the arm and whispered something into his ear. She started pulling him away from the group.

"He's drunk as a skunk," said Michelle.

"As drunk as *I* want to be," said Danny.

"Turn up the music!" somebody yelled from out of the darkness, and seconds later, Led Zeppelin's "Whole Lotta Love" wailed louder from the boom box on the log somewhere off to my right. I finished the beer I was drinking and reached for another. Energy was crackling in the air like electricity before a lightning storm, and I was caught up in it. I wanted to erase Tyler disappearing into the darkness with his arm around Jane Ratherford's waist. I wanted to forget it wasn't me he wanted to be with.

An hour passed. Then two more. I finished one beer and found another and then another. The music throbbed like a wildly beating heart. Hendrix's "Purple Haze," Black Sabbath's "Evil Woman," Melanie's "Ruby Tuesday," the Guess Who's "American Woman," the Rolling Stones' "Paint It Black." A girl started dancing barefoot in the sand. Others joined in until the beach was a swaying mass of bodies and flashes of colour in the firelight. Procol Harum slowed the pace as the opening licks to "A Whiter Shade of Pale" rolled across the beach. I focused suddenly on a swirling tangle of blonde hair, gyrating hips, and a familiar red caftan that twirled like a veil, alive in the shifting light of the fire's flames. Candy had arrived, head thrown back, one hand holding a half-full glass, the other swinging sandals in the air by the straps; flashes of silver when her bracelets caught the glow of the fire.

"Look at her," said Elizabeth into my shoulder. "She's tripping on something."

I'd gotten tired of standing and had found a spot on the log nearest to the fire. Elizabeth had settled in beside me. She'd been dancing with Danny and her breath came in warm, shallow pants against my neck.

I didn't answer. My eyes did a slow search of the darkness. We weren't the only ones watching Candy dancing. Other eyes turned from beyond the rim of the fire pit. Candy didn't notice, or if she did, she didn't care. Maybe she liked all those people watching her. She spun in slow circles and wove through the other dancers who parted in her path. Her body twisted and turned, reminding me of a cobra swaying in time to a piper's flute, her arms undulating above her head in time to the music, her skirt rising and falling on her hips. Her bare feet dug into the sand as she spun and worked her way towards the edge of the group. Each step took her that much closer to the fire. She stepped neatly around a log, changing direction slightly so that she was directly in William's line of vision, just a few feet away from him.

My brother had been standing at the edge of the firelight where the shadows were licked with the glow of orange flames. He'd been standing stock still, watching Candy's slow dance across the sand. I looked past her to look into my brother's face. I glimpsed his eyes for an instant, and I was startled by their intensity. They reflected gold and amber in the firelight, and they were fixed on Candy as if nobody else existed.

She can't be the one who broke his heart. It can't be her.

Candy moved in front of him, blocking my view. Her hips kept moving in a slow circle as she reached for my brother, her hand clutching the sandals rising to the back of his head while she flung the empty glass into the sand. Her hips ground against his and he took a step back into the shadows. She followed, all writhing hips and swaying red dress, and as I watched, her lips reached up and found his mouth. They stood locked that way for what seemed a long time before they stepped back into the shadows and the darkness swallowed them up. I turned toward Elizabeth. She was leaning forward and staring into the darkness with me. Her eyes were huge in the orangey glow of the flames.

"I can't believe what I just saw," she said. "Oh my god, she's one piece of work. A girl could take lessons."

"I need something to drink," I said. I stood and fell forward. Elizabeth grabbed my arm.

"Let's go home. What you actually need is to find your bed."

"If you say so...." my words came out slurred and my stomach did a back flip. "I don't feel so good," I said.

Elizabeth got a firmer grip around my waist. "Let's get you home, little cousin, or at least away from here. If we're sneaky enough, your father will never know you just drank enough beer to sink the *Titanic*. Count yourself lucky I've had my fill of this party too."

"You're the best, Lizbeth," I mumbled, and for that instant, I meant it because she was going to save my hide. "Let's get this ship on the road."

We started stumbling away from the water into the darker part of the beach. I thought I heard someone call my name, but Elizabeth refused to stop for me to see who it was. I thought later that it was Gideon I'd seen standing near the pine trees, but Elizabeth said I was hallucinating. The night had become a blur. The last thing I remembered was bending over in the bushes to throw up while Elizabeth held me by the shirt to keep me from tumbling in after it.

When I next came to, I was lying in my bed with the walls spinning around me and Elizabeth snoring softly from across the room. I groaned and tried to close my eyes. It felt like bits of sand had ground their way into my eyelids. Maybe I'd grown a tumour in my head. If I was lucky, it would explode and the throbbing would stop. I moaned as quietly as I could and flung an arm over my eyes. I wanted to sleep, to shut off my brain, but sleep didn't come because no matter how hard I tried, I couldn't shake the picture from my mind — Candy and William fused onto each other, their mouths together, my brother's eyes closed, his face contorted in pain. Could they have started something in Toronto? Was Candy really in love with Johnny as she'd told me, or had that been a lie?

I rubbed my temples and begged for oblivion, anything to stop the pain behind my eyes. I groaned again and rolled out of bed to stagger to the bathroom to find Aspirin and a wet facecloth. I fell back into my bed after taking two pills, with the cold cloth wrapped around my forehead. I slept for a bit, but not deeply.

When I next opened my eyes and looked at the clock, it was five a.m. I rolled onto my side and stared at the moonlight streaming onto the floor through the open window. The room was still spinning, but it had settled from a nauseous whirl into a gentle roll. Elizabeth must have opened the window as wide as she could before getting into bed, and a breeze was making the curtains billow into the room. I rolled onto my side to get the cool air full in my face. I was awake enough to run the events of the night through my head. There was so much I didn't understand, but it all seemed to come down to the question that kept bouncing around my brain. Why was Candy Parsens making out with my brother like they had a history together when he'd told me he'd never met her or Johnny before?

By the time I made my way downstairs the next morning, breakfast was over and nobody was around. I drank a big glass of water, then poured a bowl of Cheerios and loaded it up with sugar and milk before going into the store to find my mother. She wasn't behind the counter but I found her sitting on the front steps reading Elizabeth's copy of *Love Story*. She smiled sheepishly when I sat down beside her as she closed the book.

"I'm not sure why I'm reading this fluff, except it was lying on the counter in the kitchen and I happened to pick it up."

"No need to explain," I said as I tried to push Cheerios down into the milk with the back of my spoon. They didn't want to stay down. They were doing the same thing in my stomach. "I'm surprised Elizabeth let it out of her sight. She's got a thing about that book. Where is she, by the way?" I looked around.

"Out for a walk with Danny somewhere and said she'd be back soon. She seems to be making friends."

Making *out* with my friend more like. "Yeah, she's doing okay." I hesitated. "Mom, do you think Johnny and Candy Parsons fit in here at Cedar Lake?" It wasn't what I wanted to ask, but it was all I could think of. The thought of Candy and my brother gnawed away at me, a worry bead I couldn't put my finger on. My mother and Johnny had earned a worry bead of their own, but that was harder to ask about.

Mom looked at me. "Why do you ask that? I don't know Candy at all. Johnny used to live here a long time ago ...." her voice drifted away as if she didn't have the energy to finish what she was saying. Her eyes slid away from mine and focused on something in the distance.

I repositioned my knees sideways so they were resting against her leg. "Last night, at the beach, Candy seemed to know William. I don't know where or how, but they seemed to know each other pretty well. I couldn't figure it out."

"Candy and William?" Mom frowned. "He never mentioned anything to me about knowing Candy. I thought it was just Johnny." She clamped her mouth shut.

"Where is William today?" I asked, looking around the yard as if I might find him hiding behind a tree.

"He's driven with your dad to Campbellford to pick up some supplies. They should be back mid-afternoon."

"And I know you've been seeing Johnny," I blurted out. I immediately felt miserable. I lowered my head so that my hair fell across my eyes.

Mom was silent for a moment. "Johnny just needs somebody to talk to, that's all it is. You can't go reading too much into things, Darlene." Her voice held a warning and a hint of fear, or perhaps I was imagining that too.

"I just don't know why they're here." I was grumpy. I wanted answers and I was getting none. The secrets were starting to weigh on me.

Mom rested her warm hand against my cheek. "You are too impatient, my girl." She lowered her hand to her lap. Her voice was wistful. "I remember what it was like to be your age waiting for my life to begin. I wanted it all. I thought I had all the answers and that I could control my life." She paused and her smile was gentle. "Just be careful not to jump in too fast. Everything will unfold in time, Darlene. Enjoy your summer and don't fret about things that aren't your concern."

I felt Mom's leg pull away from mine and heard the screen door snap back into place after she'd gone into the store. I stared up through the branches of the trees and watched the flickers of sunlight all shimmery and golden on the top side of the leaves with the bottoms shaded and dark. Perhaps the answers were somewhere up there, waiting to sift through the foliage. What was my mother trying to tell me? To trust her? To turn the other way when I saw her with Johnny? If only it were that easy. I couldn't get past Johnny's eyes as he'd searched for my mother in the store and the disappointment when he'd found me instead.

I spent the morning typing in my room. After lunch, I biked over to Gideon's. He was sitting at his typewriter, a freshly brewed pot of tea, a jug of milk, and two mugs waiting on the coffee table, as if he knew I'd be there in time to join him. After I poured us each a cup, I plopped myself down on the couch and Gideon swung his chair around to face me.

"So what's up, Little Fin? You look like something has upset you."

"I'm fine. Just fine. What're you working on?" I asked.

"The column. Another anti-war rant."

"You wouldn't want to know what my father thinks of people who don't support the war. He believes Canada should stand shoulder to shoulder with the U.S. in Vietnam. He thinks our prime minister Trudeau represents all that is wrong with today's youth, that he's little better than a Communist."

"Your father has a right to his point of view. It may be narrow and ill-informed, but he's certainly entitled to have it." Gideon's shrewd eyes studied me. "Where do you stand on the issue?"

"I don't know why people just can't get along. What's the point of killing each other when there's enough to go around for everyone?"

"Out of the mouths of babes," murmured Gideon. "But you know it's not that simple. You always have to question and dig deeper than what you read in the press."

"I know. I know. Different ideologies. Power struggles. Greed. Killing innocent people in the name of war. My Lai should never have happened."

"That is an ugly stain on the American cause, no doubt about it. We haven't heard the last of that travesty yet." His eyes brightened as if he saw something I didn't.

"Will there be a trial?"

"Most certainly. The outcome will depend on who talks. The army isn't known for turning on its own. The media has to get the story out. I believe that with every ounce of my journalistic blood. We need to provoke. Some might tell you being a reporter is not an honorable profession, but I tell you it is the most noble when done with a social conscience. The army will fight to keep this story from gaining momentum. It's our job to make sure it does."

"Those American soldiers killed the whole village. Women and children. They threw their bodies into a big pit. How could the army pretend that never happened?"

"Is that a rhetorical question? How could the U.S. stay in a war they cannot win?"

I was suddenly impatient with this never-ending debate that had no answers.

"I thought I saw you last night," I said.

"I took Ruby for a walk — perhaps you saw me then."

"Were you near Minnow Beach?"

"No, I didn't get that far."

"I thought I saw you standing in the pines near the beach. William came home for the weekend."

"I heard. What is bothering you, Darlene? Your thoughts are jumping around like fleas on a dog."

The ringing of the phone saved me from answering. Gideon picked up the receiver but kept his eyes on my face. I grabbed a *National Geographic* from a stack on the coffee table and pretended to read.

"Are you sure? I waited for you, but … no, no. That's all right. We can reschedule." Gideon was sitting up straighter with his head cocked to one side, listening intently. "I'm really interested …. Okay, but anytime, anywhere you say." He listened to the voice at the other end and kept trying to interrupt. He lifted his free hand in surrender. "If that's what you want. Thanks for letting me know."

Gideon clunked down the receiver. I looked up from the magazine.

"What's going on?" I asked.

His eyes were staring at the wall as if he was watching something far away. It took a bit before he looked at me. "I had a lead for a story I've been working on and wanted to get published soon. The information that a secret source promised me was going to make it an international scoop. Now, it's back to the drawing board."

"What story?"

"Oh, one about the war." He said it like his mind was on something else. "Damnation," he said under his breath.

"Maybe I could help get the information for you. Who's your source?"

Gideon focused his eyes on me as if remembering I was there. "I'll have to swear you to secrecy. You wouldn't be able to tell anybody else, not even your mother."

I made a cross over my heart. "Promise," I said, "and hope to die."

Gideon stared at me until he seemed satisfied. "Okay. You are a journalist in training and must abide by our creed to protect our sources at all costs. Candy Parsens called me the morning of the beach party and said she had something for me about Vietnam. The My Lai massacre to be exact."

"Candy? Are you sure she's telling the truth?" I said it without thinking then looked down at the magazine in my lap so that Gideon wouldn't see my eyes. Candy had secrets. She liked to be on display. I liked listening to her stories, but how could they all be true? "Maybe you should be careful about what she tells you, Gideon."

"You'll miss out on the best scoops if you aren't willing to get your hands a little dirty. Besides, she told me she had documents. I'd like you to go track her down and try to get her to talk. This story is one that potentially could show the world how the American army and government cover up what's been going on in Vietnam. It's a story that needs to be told." His expression was a mixture of excitement and frustration.

"I'll try, Gideon." I stood up quickly and started for the door. "I'll get on it right away."

"Come back right after you speak with her," he called to me. "Don't let me down on this one, Little Fin."

I opened the front door and looked back. Gideon was leaning back in his chair with his eyes closed and a big smile on his face. He was probably thinking about having his story run in the *New York Times* and the *Washington Post*. He was salivating to win the Pulitzer for journalism. I hoped Candy wasn't leading him on about the documents.

I wanted to talk to her for my own reasons. Beginning with why William was making out with her when he said he didn't know her. I saw the way he'd looked at her when she was walking across the sand. I was sure he'd known her from before. I had to get home and talk to William before he left for Toronto. I wanted to find out what he knew about Candy before I went to talk to her.

Elizabeth was waiting for me on the front steps. She met me halfway up the path. Her hair was loose and soft, shining a dull gold in the sunlight. I pushed kinky strands of mine out of my face and scowled.

"There's the party animal. You look like death," she said. "Like someone drained all the blood out of your face. That is except for your eyes. They're red as tomatoes."

"Thanks."

"Your mom's been looking for you. William is splitting this groovy scene."

"Are they inside?"

"Yeah."

The screen door creaked open and we both turned as William emerged onto the top step. He was carrying his duffel bag and a bag of cookies. Mom followed behind him, and he turned and hugged her. She looked at us over his shoulder.

"There you are, Darlene," said Mom. "I was hoping you'd make it back in time to say goodbye to your brother."

I looked up at William. His aviator sunglasses hid his eyes. His beard was growing scraggly so his face was dark and rough-looking. He gave my mother one last hug before bounding down the stairs towards us.

"See you," he said.

"Will you be back this summer?" Elizabeth asked. She took a couple of steps towards him so that she was directly in his path. Her hands were holding onto her waist and she stood so that one hip jutted out. She was wearing a white cotton blouse and pink hot pants. When she looked at William, she opened her eyes wide and pouted.

"Maybe next weekend. I promised Mom I'd help her with stock. Later, Elizabeth." He stepped around her and kept walking.

I glared at Elizabeth behind her back and fell into step alongside William as he headed toward his car, a second-hand Volkswagen Beetle he'd bought the summer before. When I thought we were out of earshot of Elizabeth, I said, "I saw you with Candy Parsens last night at the beach."

William turned to stare down at me through his glasses. His eyes were shadowy circles behind the dark lenses. "As I remember, you were in no condition to see anything clearly last night."

"I know what I saw."

"What you think you saw."

"What I know I saw. Elizabeth saw you too."

"Give it a rest. My love life is none of your business."

"So you *do* know Candy." I stood in front of the driver's door so William couldn't get around me. "What's going on between you two?"

"Mom's watching. Get out of my way."

"No."

"Don't make me have to move you."

"How do you know Candy?"

William looked toward the house. "Johnny, all right? I know Johnny and Candy from Toronto." William waved in the direction of Mom and Elizabeth. "See you next weekend!" he called. "Now get out of my way. I'm already late."

I stepped aside. William pulled hard on the door and it swung wide open, pushing him back. He got inside and started the engine, then rolled down the window. When he looked up at me, he let the muscles in his face go slack. "It was nothing, okay?"

"So why did you lie about knowing them?"

"Because I didn't want to have to get into it with you." He smiled, his lopsided, little-boy grin, before laying one arm across the back of the car seat and turning to back onto the street. "See you next weekend, kid."

I stood in the driveway and watched William drive too fast away from me down toward the highway, his old car burning oil that left a trail of black smoke in the air after he'd disappeared from view. I walked back to the store, kicking at a stone on the path.

Something was going on. I could feel it in my journalistic bones.

I promised Mom I wouldn't be long and biked over to Candy's. The flower power van was in the driveway, but the house had that empty feel it gets when people have been gone a while.

I left my bike leaning against the rain barrel and climbed down to the beach. After I'd sat in the sand and contemplated life, I waded around the point to the stretch of sand where Candy and I'd spent the afternoon. I couldn't see any sign of her. I picked up a stick lying next to a piece of driftwood and poked holes in the sand as I followed the beach along the shoreline. I reached the path and climbed it up to the road. I walked along the bluff to the point that overlooked the beach. An adult and a child were playing in the sand near the shore. At first I thought it was Candy with Sean but that was just because I wanted it to be. I started down the path that snaked through the woods down to the north end of the beach.

I must have been delusional not to have recognized Johnny the first time I looked. He was dressed in cutoff shorts and wasn't wearing a shirt. I didn't go any further than the edge of the sand, watching for a while from behind a tree. Sean was digging with a shovel and filling a plastic yellow pail that he'd carry over to Johnny and dump on his feet. Johnny was building a sandcastle just out of reach of the waves that rolled across the sand. I was close enough to see the green eagle on his biceps move up and down as he worked. They kept at it for a while until Johnny stood and stretched. Then he bent and swung Sean in the air over his head, turning in a circle and spinning him around and around. Sean squealed the whole time and called, "Daddy, Daddy! Airplane!" Johnny pulled him close and ran into the water, splashing and dunking Sean up to his waist before lifting him into the air. I could hear Sean's laughter as I turned to go.

I walked out of the woods and onto the road, starting slowly back to get my bike. Johnny was looking less and less like the bad person I wanted him to be. If he was a bad person, then my mother would see through him. My father would stand a chance.

There was still no sign of Candy at their house. I looked in the back yard and then got on my bike. As I pedalled toward the road, I thought about Sean. The whole time I'd seen him with Candy, I'd never once heard him laugh like he just had with Johnny. Candy had never once swung him around and around in the air, pretending that he could fly.

It was nearly three o'clock when I started up the driveway to the store. Dad's car was still in the driveway, but he'd be going back to Ottawa soon. He always left at two thirty exactly. He said he had to get back to the city while it was still light. You could set your watch by his leaving, so today was strange.

I was dragging my feet, not really wanting to talk to anybody, when I heard Mom's voice. She and Dad were sitting on the steps next to each other and they didn't see me. I stepped back behind Dad's car. Maybe I'd just stay out of their way until he left. Their voices got louder and I looked back. They'd left the steps and had started walking toward the car. They still hadn't seen me and I don't know why, but I stayed out of sight and watched them. If I wasn't careful, I was going to turn into a creepy voyeur.

"Where did you go last night?" Mom asked.

"I couldn't sleep, so I went outside for a bit of air. Didn't want to disturb you." Dad had stopped walking and was looking down at Mom's bowed head.

"I woke up around one thirty and you were gone. Are you having trouble sleeping again?" she asked.

"Lately, yeah. It's been ten years but it feels like yesterday sometimes."

Mom reached up and cupped her hand around my dad's cheek. He closed his eyes and his head seemed to melt into her hand. He hadn't shaved and his face looked grizzly and tired. They stood that way for a while.

Mom lowered her hand. She asked, "Is it time to see the doctor? Your headaches are getting worse."

Dad shook his head. "I'll be all right. It's just this time of year. Brings it back."

"I know," said Mom. "I know." She put her arm through his and they started walking with their heads down in my direction. "But you can't let this go. I'll phone if you like."

I slipped behind the birch trees and through the woods. When I was close to the road, I started running. I didn't stop until I'd reached the beach and scrambled up the rocks to my lookout. My breath was coming in ragged tears that hurt my lungs. I sat there for a long time, getting calm and watching the waves and thinking about my dead sister Annie. I didn't want to think about her, but I couldn't stop myself from seeing her face. Dad's words had brought her back.

She'd been seven when she'd drowned. If she'd lived, she'd be turning seventeen on Monday. We'd be celebrating her birthday with a big cake and presents and a family dinner. I wiped my hair out of my eyes and focused on the far shore.

I remembered snippets of Annie, frames frozen in time that would come back to me sometimes. Sitting next to her in the hammock, our legs and arms pressed warm against each other, looking at my favourite picture book, *Pokey the Flying Rabbit*; watching out the front window for her to come home from school so we could play; sitting between Annie and William in the back seat of our car on the way to Sunday school singing "Jesus Loves Me." Annie had been tiny for her age, with brown hair and eyes like my mom. She always wore her hair in pigtails and had black patent leather shoes that I envied with all my heart. I don't know if these memories of how she looked were first-hand or formed from the snapshots in our photograph album. I remembered the shoes, though. Annie used to wear them skipping on the driveway, and I was jealous of those shoes. I never knew what happened to them after.

My last memory of Annie was of her wearing a red and gold striped bathing suit when Dad carried her out of the lake. Her arms and legs had swung like a rag doll's, and her hair was all tangled with a trail of something green and slimy across her cheek. I don't know why I have this image locked in my head — Dad crying, great heaving sobs with his mouth wide open and his eyes shut, walking towards us with Annie in his arms — but it is always with me, just beneath the surface, waiting until I am overtired or feeling low. It appears as I am drifting off to sleep or when the first fingers of sun are sliding across the ceiling. Some nights, I wake up calling out for Annie, panicked that I won't be able to find her. I've never told anybody about the dream. They all think I've forgotten. I want it that way.

William told me that I'd taken one look at Dad holding Annie's body and started running the other way. It took them an hour to find me. I don't remember. I didn't remember anything before or after that day or for a long time afterwards. They tell me I was the reason Dad wasn't watching her, the reason he was distracted. I was throwing a tantrum and he was trying to get me to stop screaming. I might have been, but to me, it's just a story.

The wind had come up, and my hair was blowing around my face. A cloud blew in front of the sun and the beach was suddenly in shadow. I closed my eyes and lay back on my big flat rock and stared up into the sky. I lay like that for a while, and when the sun came out again I stood up and spread my arms wide, holding my face upwards to look above the lake and the long dark line of spruce trees. I yelled at the top of my lungs into the sky and let the wind whip away my words. "Happy Birthday, Annie. I hope you're doing okay wherever you are. I hope you've forgiven me."

Chapter Eleven

T HE NEXT DAY, I helped Mom in the store. I kept looking out the window, hoping to see Candy, but there was no sign of her. Mom finally let me go after lunch. On my way to Gideon's, I biked over to the Davidsons' to find Candy. I knew Gideon would be pacing his office waiting impatiently for me to bring some news for his story.

Bobby opened the door. He was scratching his bare chest and looked like he'd just woken up, even though it was after lunch. His Afro was wild and matted on one side. An unlit cigarette hung from the side of his mouth.

"You looking for Candy? She's gone to Toronto for a couple of days. I'm watching the kid until Johnny gets back from the store. You wanna come in and hang with me?"

Toronto? "No, that's okay. Who did she go to Toronto with?"

"She took the bus, I think."

I was backing away without realizing it until I stumbled on the bottom step. Bobby laughed. "Sure you don't want to come in and keep me company, baby? I don't bite. I'm a friendly kind of guy."

"No, I have to go."

I turned and started running toward my bike leaning against the rain barrel. Bobby's laughter chased me down the driveway.

That afternoon, Gideon moved from tea to whiskey as the hour hand passed two. He'd made me an iced tea from shiny crystals he kept in a round green tin in the cupboard over the stove. The mixture was root beer brown and rolled sickly sweet on my tongue.

"Why would she go to Toronto now?" I asked for about the tenth time since I'd gotten there.

Gideon took a long swallow before setting the tumbler next to his typewriter. He'd been ignoring me while he typed out an article for his column, but now he was done.

"No idea. She must have changed her mind about telling that story."

"Maybe she won't be coming back," I said. "She told me she would probably just up and leave one day."

"Well, so much for my Pulitzer." Gideon held up a hand. "Listen," he said. He leaned over and turned up the volume on the radio beside his desk.

"… found dead in a bathtub in Paris, France. Cause of death unknown at this point. A great loss to the world of music."

"Who, Gideon? Who died?"

"Jim Morrison of the Doors. You know, 'Light My Fire.' I remember seeing him perform that song on the Ed Sullivan show. He was supposed to change the lyric from 'Girl, we couldn't get much higher' to 'Girl, we couldn't get much better.' Anyhow, Morrison stuck with the original lyric and Sullivan was so mad he wouldn't even shake Morrison's hand." Gideon chuckled before his face turned serious. "He was too young by half. Joplin, Hendrix, now Morrison. The drug culture keeps taking the most talented. Remember this date, kid. July third, 1971. It'll be famous for all the wrong reasons."

"Candy said she knew him."

"Really? I guess it's possible."

"Anything's possible," I said.

"If Candy's gone for a while, or maybe for good, we need to come up with a new plan of attack," wheezed Gideon before he bent over coughing. It took him a while to catch his breath. His face had turned a light shade of plum before he finally started talking again. He held the glass to his lips and took another deep swallow. He turned away from me as he set the glass on the desk. He wiped his forehead with the bottom of his shirt before he faced me again. "I'm still shaking this round of bronchitis and I need you to be my eyes and ears. Johnny's in the thick of this story. I want you to go over and interview him."

"He's not going to share anything with me. I can tell you that right now."

"He will after I call him."

"What will you say?"

"Just leave it to me. He'll talk."

"Should I take notes?"

"Yeah. This can be part of your article on people at the lake. Find out some of the background stuff and anything personal he can tell you. I want your impressions. See if you can get him talking about Vietnam. Don't push too hard, but lead him there whenever you get the chance. I also want you to take a look around. Try to find those papers Candy was talking about."

"That sounds ... illegal."

"Well, she did offer them, so it's not like you'd be stealing anything."

"How will I know what papers I'm looking for?"

"They'll have to do with the Vietnam War. They'll probably look official, maybe even military documents."

"I don't know, Gideon."

"It'll be fine. Trust me. Finish your drink and by the time you get to Johnny's, he'll be ready to give an interview. You'll have to come up with a reason to look around. Use your imagination."

I watched Gideon over the rim of my glass as I took another swallow of iced tea. He was smiling and rubbed his beard up and down like he did when something made him happy. "Nothing like a good story to get the blood up," he said before emptying the last of his glass. The colour was gone from his face and his skin looked greyish in the light from his desk lamp.

"Are you feeling okay, Gideon? Maybe you need a different medicine."

"Don't worry about me, Little Fin. I'm getting along just fine. Everything is unfolding as it should."

When I left Gideon's, the landscape had darkened under the belly of swollen clouds, and rumbles of thunder were growing louder until they seemed to be just over-head. I hadn't brought a jacket and by the time I reached Johnny's driveway the rain was falling in wind-whipped sheets. My hair was dripping and my shirt and shorts felt cold and clammy against my skin. I was happy to see Johnny's van in the driveway and pedalled faster through the rain toward the cottage. A green car with Pennsylvania plates was in front of the van. I'd never seen the car before and biked up close to it to look inside. I rubbed moisture from the window with the palm of my hand. The back seat was littered with styrofoam cups and food wrappers, but nothing that let me know who owned it.

I left my bike leaning against a tree and stood shivering on the back stoop as I waited for Johnny to answer the door. A jagged shaft of lightning flashed above the tree line followed by a crash of thunder, making me jump. I raised my hand again to pound on the door when it suddenly swung open beneath my fist.

"Come in then," said Johnny. His black eyes drilled into mine as if he was trying to glare me off the top step. He was wiping his hands on a tea towel, and I could smell bread baking in the oven. He turned back toward the counter while I followed, surveying the kitchen as I went. I blinked a few times. The mess from my last visit had been cleared away, except for the dishes he'd used to make the bread dough. Even the garbage had been removed, and the kitchen table was empty of dishes.

I sat down in a chair at the end of the table where I could watch Johnny filling the sink with soapy water. He was dressed in torn jeans and a white cotton shirt with red flowers woven into the collar. His feet were bare. The yellow light from the swag lamp with pink tassels above the sink pooled around his dark hair like a halo.

"Is Sean sleeping?" I asked.

"He's been down awhile. He should be waking soon." Johnny started putting the dishes into the sink and turned his back on me. "Bobby told me you were by earlier."

"Yeah. I see his car's gone."

"He and Kirk drove into Campbellford."

I pulled my notebook from my soggy knapsack. The cover was stained brown and damp, but it had protected the pages inside. "I'm helping Gideon. He was supposed to call to arrange an interview for an article and ..." I couldn't finish my thought. I felt awkward being there, knowing Johnny was interested in my mom.

"Like I told Gideon, I'll answer a few questions for your article since Candy's in Toronto. I have to say that I was a little surprised to hear she'd promised Gideon an interview."

So that's how Gideon got Johnny to talk to me. Candy really must know something that Johnny didn't want me to find out. I lowered my head so he wouldn't see my face turn red. I asked, "How long have you known Candy?"

"A long time. We grew up together and were going to get married."

"You were going to marry Frances, right?" I scratched a few words on the pad.

"I've never heard of any Frances."

I lifted my head and stared at him. "Candy told me Frances was her sister." *And Sean's mother.*

Johnny laughed. "What else did she tell you?"

"That she knew Jim Morrison. He died yesterday."

"Yeah, I just heard on the radio that he OD'd. It's hard to believe. It's even harder to believe Candy knew him."

"She also said you were a pilot in Vietnam." *Shut up* I told myself, *or Johnny's going to figure out that you've already interviewed Candy.*

He dropped his head until his hair covered his face. When he looked at me again, he was smiling. It didn't reach his eyes. "I was, but Gideon told me your article was about newcomers to the lake and our impressions. I'd rather you not mention my name. I don't need that kind of ego shit."

"I'll just have you as an unnamed source."

"As long as we're clear on that." He stood and headed over to the sink. His hands rested on the counter when he looked out the window. "Looks like the rain is letting up."

"What do you think of Cedar Lake?"

"It's cool. I like being away from the city. Life is simple here. Waking up to the water and clean air is a bonus."

"You met my mother before you came to Cedar Lake." I trained my eyes on his back and waited.

Johnny kept resting his weight on the counter. He turned his head to look at me. "My parents owned a cottage here years ago. Your mother was a few years older than me, but I remember her. I met your brother in a Toronto restaurant. We just struck up a conversation and realized we had a connection. I thought Candy and Sean might like to spend the summer here."

"Where in Toronto?"

"Yorkville."

William had told me he liked to hang out in Yorkville. Maybe Johnny was telling the truth. "So you lived in Toronto before you came to Cedar Lake for the summer."

"Yeah."

"But you come from the States —" I let the sentence hang unfinished.

"I decided to move to Canada after I left the air force. I just wanted a change of scene. Cedar Lake is as far from the rat race as you can get. We love it here."

"What was it like in Vietnam?"

"It was what it was. Just a memory now. Something I'm not too eager to talk about."

Sorry, Gideon. I put my book and pen back in my knapsack. "Do you mind if I use your washroom?" I asked as I straightened up. Gideon's iced tea was pressing on my bladder, and I was out of questions. I probably hadn't asked any of the right ones.

"Go ahead. It's upstairs at the end of the hall."

"I know. We used to come for supper when the Davidsons were here other summers."

I climbed the stairs and started down the dark corridor. The carpet was gritty with beach sand. Dust swirled in the greyish light, reminding me of Candy and how she hadn't cared what the house looked like. Johnny hadn't made it this far in cleaning up the mess that she'd let accumulate, although the hose of a Hoover vacuum rested against the wall at the end of the hallway. I passed a closed door where Sean must be sleeping and reached the second bedroom. The door was partially closed, but I pushed it open and looked inside. I could hear Johnny in the kitchen. I figured I had a few seconds to look for documents before he got suspicious.

Light filtered through the slats of a blind and layered the room in shades of grey. Rain had splashed onto the floor through the open window, and gusts of wind made the metal blind rattle against the glass. The bed wasn't made — the covers pushed aside and draped half on the floor, a wet towel tossed on the pillow. A stack of Johnny's clothes was on a chair beside the dresser. The dresser top was littered in silver and gold bracelets, brightly coloured scarves, bottles of face cream, perfume and make up, some of which was spilled across the oak surface. The scent of Tabu was all around me, as if Candy were hiding behind the door, ready to jump into the room at any moment with her happy smile and arms wide to hug me. I stepped closer and skirted around the bed. A large black suitcase stood open on the floor, its back resting against the bed frame, half-filled with Johnny's T-shirts and jeans. Next to it was his shaving kit and a box of clean towels and Sean's clothes. It looked like Johnny wasn't planning to hang around much longer. I wondered if he planned to wait for Candy. She'd left too many of her things not to be coming back.

I quickly backed out of the room and pulled the door back the way I'd found it. I didn't think it would be a good idea to let Johnny know I'd figured out he was going somewhere. A happy thought flashed in my mind. If he left, he'd be leaving my mother alone. She might be sad for a while, but she'd be okay. She'd get over him. She had to.

I tried to walk quietly down the hall to the bathroom, but the wooden floor under the carpet creaked with each footstep. Every noise made me cringe. I reached the bathroom at last and had my hand on the doorknob when I heard a noise behind me. It was coming from the spare bedroom across the hall. I froze and looked over my shoulder in time to see the door slide shut and the doorknob rotate slowly into place. Somebody was inside the bedroom — somebody who'd been watching me. I remembered the green car in the driveway. Did Johnny have somebody in there he didn't want anybody to see?

It would have been easy for me to cross the hall and pull the door wide open, but I wasn't that brave. In fact, I was as scared as I got watching horror movies, sitting in a darkened theatre. I didn't need to go to the bathroom that bad. I turned and jogged toward the stairs, not caring about the noise or the cloud of dust that swirled around my feet.

~••~

I found my mother in the store, counting the money in the till as she got ready to lock up for the night. I raced up to the bathroom then back into the store, where I waited for her to finish rolling coins into brown wrappers. She shook her head when I offered to help. I wandered around the aisles straightening boxes of cereal and bags of chips and figuring out what I would say to her about Johnny. Finally, she called me over.

"You look like you got caught in the rain by the state of your hair. Where've you been?" Mom asked. "I could have used you today."

"Sorry, Mom. I was helping Gideon with a story."

She frowned at me. "Darlene, you have to stop this roaming around like you haven't any responsibilities. Your father believes we have to make you buckle down, and I'm beginning to think he might be right."

I stood without answering, my eyes lowered.

"I want you to look after the store tomorrow. I'm going into Toronto for the day."

My heart quickened. I raised my head. "By yourself?"

"No, with a friend. We're getting an early start, so you'll have to open up for me. Plan to spend your day working. No wandering off."

"I wish I could come with you."

Mom's eyes softened. "It's not possible, but maybe another time. I'll make sure we have a girls' day out before summer is over."

"Who are you going to Toronto with tomorrow?" I asked.

Mom started walking toward the front door. "A friend. I just … I just need a day away. Get a good night's sleep," she called. "I'm counting on you to look after things tomorrow. Please throw the deadbolt behind me. I have an errand to run. I'll come in the back door."

"Okay," I said as the door slammed shut behind her.

Does Dad know you're going to Toronto with just a friend? Would this friend already have his suitcase packed to go with you?

I kicked the closed door with my foot. What was left of my family was falling apart. I had no idea what to do.

Elizabeth woke me when she tripped on the rug and banged her knee on the side of my bed. If that noise hadn't woken me, her stream of curse words made sure. When she saw I was awake, she dropped down onto the edge of my bed and rubbed her leg. I'd forgotten to close the curtains and could make out her dark silhouette hovering above me like an evil spirit.

"Where've you been?" I asked.

"Babysitting, and I have to tell you, I'm getting tired of you never being around to take the calls. You owe me."

"You're awfully late." I rolled around her to squint at the clock. It was going on two a.m.

"They went to play cards and forgot the time." She shrugged. "More money for me."

I propped myself up on an elbow. "I have to look after the store tomorrow. Mom's going to Toronto for the day."

"*She is?* Maybe I can get a ride with her. I'd so like to get out of here, even if it's just for one day."

I smiled. Elizabeth would make my mother think twice about going off with Johnny. Elizabeth was the perfect solution. "You'll have to get up early. I think she's leaving before seven."

Elizabeth groaned and stood up. "I'll set my alarm and catch her before she goes. Maybe I'll talk my old man into letting me stay home for the rest of the summer."

"What about the car he promised if you lasted here?"

Elizabeth tossed her hair back and looked down at me. "I'm hoping I can talk him into letting me stay home *and* get the car. He's probably fed up with Mom pestering him and will be delighted to have me back."

"How is your mom?"

Elizabeth didn't say anything for a bit. She was turned away from me now and her voice came out smaller. "I wanted her to come with me for the summer, but she wouldn't leave Toronto. I have no idea what she's hanging on to there. It's not like my father wants her to stay."

"I'm sorry, Elizabeth."

I could see her looking down at me. "So am I. I guess you and me aren't all that different, are we, Dar? I mean, when it comes to having parents who don't have their shit together."

"No, maybe not."

Elizabeth crossed over to her bed and I watched her pull her shirt over her head before I turned onto my other side and stared at the wall.

~●●~

I heard Elizabeth's alarm go off but I rolled over and went back to sleep. When I finally opened my eyes, the birds had started singing crazy songs to each other outside the window and the sun was partway up. Disoriented for a moment, I rolled onto my side and stared over at Elizabeth's bed. I expected to see the covers pushed back and Elizabeth gone. It was a shock to see blonde hair draped across her pillow. I sat up in a panic. Elizabeth had slept through her alarm and now my mother was probably halfway to Toronto without her.

I jumped out of bed and scrambled into my clothes, leaping across the room and bolting down the stairs, searching for my mother, trying to reach her in time.

I was too late.

Her note with instructions for the day and a key to the cash register lay on the kitchen table under the salt shaker. I grabbed the paper and studied her words, trying to read something hidden between the lines. It was hopeless. She'd gone off for the day with Johnny and I had no reason to think she'd be coming back.

Chapter Twelve

ELIZABETH CAME INTO the shop just after lunch. Her face reminded me of a hornet that had been poked with a stick.

"I can't believe you didn't wake me up. You knew how bad I wanted out of here."

"I didn't know you'd slept through your alarm. It wasn't like I wanted you to miss the trip to Toronto."

"What a bloody stupid day. I have to find a way back to Toronto before I go out of my mind." Elizabeth wandered over to the front door. She stared at me before turning and leaning into the screen. She pressed her face into the mesh. "I just want some excitement. Is that too damn much to ask?"

I went and stood next to her. "You could always catch the bus to Toronto. Candy did the other day."

Elizabeth turned sideways and smiled at me. "Candy. What are you doing hanging around with her? Girls like Candy were always hovering around Mick's band, trying to do something to get noticed. Groupies — who try to become important by getting their claws into someone famous. I can see her getting tired of playing wife here in dullsville."

"She just left for a few days." I didn't like how Elizabeth had described Candy, like she was a barnacle, sticking onto Johnny because she had nothing going on for herself. "Candy knew lots of famous people."

"Oh yeah, name one."

"She was best friends with Janis Joplin and Jim Morrison."

Elizabeth threw back her head and laughed. It took her a while to catch her breath. "No way. I'd bet money Candy never got within a thousand miles of Joplin or Morrison. Did she really tell you that? Even better, did you believe her?"

I nodded, but the truth was, I'd begun to doubt Candy some time ago. Could she have been making all of it up though? Couldn't she have known Janis Joplin, Mary Hopkin, Jim Morrison, and J.D. Salinger? It did sound way out there.

"Why do you think Johnny and Candy really came to Cedar Lake?" I asked.

"Maybe to escape their lives in Toronto. Who knows? Who cares?" Elizabeth pushed open the screen door. "I'm going for a walk. See you later."

I watched her cross to the path and bend to pick some daisies. She smelled them before crushing them in her hand and scattering them into the wind. I turned and went back to sit at my post behind the counter. I pulled the stool closer to the window so I could see the road. After a while, I closed my eyes and made a wish. If my mother would come home tonight, I'd stick around and help her more. I'd do anything not to have to break the news to my father that she'd gone off to Toronto without him.

Elizabeth came into the store as I was locking up for the night. She'd spent the day at the beach and was heading upstairs for a shower, a facial, and a couple of coats of pink pearl nail polish — tips she'd learned from the model Cheryl Tiegs in *Seventeen* magazine.

I stepped outside and searched the yard for signs of my mother, but she hadn't yet returned. It was too early to give up hope, but I didn't want to sit around waiting. I grabbed my notebook from under the counter and a bag of chips and headed for the beach. There were a few hours of sunlight left, and I wanted to work on my article for Gideon about life in Cedar Lake. I was almost ready to begin typing on the second-hand Olivetti my mother had given me for Christmas. I planned to bring my notes to Gideon in the morning along with the information I'd written down from my interview with Johnny. I'd tried calling Gideon a few times from the store in the afternoon, but he hadn't answered the phone. A new kid had delivered the mail all week. I figured Gideon must be taking a break from the world. He sometimes did that when he was swamped with writing projects and couldn't be bothered with people. He told me once that he'd had enough of dealing with idiots to last him two lifetimes.

~••~

This time, Tyler Livingstone was sitting on my rock wait-ing for me, and my heart gave a happy leap when I saw him. For a few seconds, I forgot about my mother and the big worry I'd been carrying around inside. Then I brought myself back to earth. I scowled and called myself stupid under my breath for thinking Tyler was interested in me. The only good thing was that he had no idea how I felt.

I climbed until my head was level with his legs. Tyler grinned at me and offered a hand to pull me up the last few feet. His touch was like a shock through my body, but I tried not to let on. *Play it cool,* I said to myself. I sat down and kept my hands busy ripping open the bag of chips I'd saved for when I was watching the sunset. I set the open bag down between us.

"Thought you'd be here tonight," he said. "I've been sitting on your rock thinking you wouldn't be able to stay away."

"You're psychic."

"Except I haven't got a clue what's coming next."

"Most psychics make up their predictions anyhow." I looked away. "The lake is calm tonight."

Tyler took his eyes off me and swivelled his head toward the beach. "It's a great view, that's for sure."

We both reached for a chip and my hand brushed against his.

"'Scuse me," he said.

"You took the chip I wanted," I said.

Tyler grinned at me. "Open wide."

I obeyed and he stuck the chip on my tongue. I chewed slowly and took a minute to study the waves rolling onto the beach and the golden light sprinkled across the water as the sun got a little lower in the sky. A wind had come up and the waves were higher than normal for this time of day. Tyler shifted backwards and leaned on his elbows.

"That woman — Candy," he said. "I saw her walking to the bus a couple of mornings ago. I was out jogging."

"So?"

"She was crying. I asked her if everything was okay. She said it was all screwed up."

"I think she and Johnny aren't getting along so well." I looked back at the lake.

"I don't remember much about that beach party the other night because I was so blasted, but I thought I saw her with your brother. I seriously think he shouldn't get tangled up with her. She's bad news."

I let my breath out slowly. "William knows her from Toronto. I think they're just friends."

"She seems pretty friendly, that's for sure," Tyler said. He was quiet for a minute, then he said, "I saw her skinny dipping a few times when I was out jogging. She was down at the point, on that little stretch of beach. She saw me, but she didn't care that I was there."

"I wonder how many others saw her too."

Tyler shrugged. "She likes to flaunt it."

"I guess." It was a disconcerting idea. Anonymous men watching and waiting. Voyeurs in the shadows, with

Candy putting on a show. I shifted uncomfortably, thinking how I'd been secretly watching people too recently.

"I like her," I said. "She seems … sad and mixed up, maybe. Like she wants to belong but doesn't fit in."

Tyler gave me his lopsided smile. "You always see the best in people, even when they don't deserve it. Take me for instance."

"Are you digging for compliments?"

"Compliments are good. I also forgot to mention you're one of the smartest girls I know. What are you working on now?" He grabbed for my notebook and had it open before I could stop him.

"Give that back."

He lifted an arm to block my hand. "Say, this isn't bad." His eyes skimmed the page. "Did I really say that?"

I made a final lunge and grabbed the book from him. "Not funny, Livingstone."

"You really can write." He studied me like he was seeing me from a new angle. "I hope we can stay friends, you know, when we're old and grey."

"Stranger things could happen."

Tyler laughed. "Well, I wanted to see you before I leave. I quit my job yesterday and I'm heading out west to visit my cousins in Calgary. My parents are always nattering at each other like a couple of fishwives and I need to get away."

"They still haven't decided about Andrew and the group home?"

Tyler shook his head. "No, but Mom will win. If not, Dad can expect his life to be hell for a very, very long time."

"I'm really sorry, Tyler."

I was sorry about Andrew but way more sorry that Tyler was leaving. The rest of the summer stretched before me, long and empty. I averted my eyes from his. Tyler reached up and pushed my hair away from my face in a motion so quick his fingers felt like feathers on my forehand. "It's a hell of a thing," he said. Then, he sat up and then pushed himself to his feet. He looked down at me. "I'll send you a letter from Calgary. I'd like to stay friends with you, Darlene. Someday, I'll say I knew you when."

"You're full of it tonight," I said and smiled at him so he knew I wasn't serious.

He took a step back and bent over me. "How about a kiss, for friends' sake, as I head off into the great big world?" He crouched down like a cat getting ready to pounce and leaned his face into mine. His mouth was so close I could taste mint on his breath. His eyes filled mine and he seemed to be trying to tell me something. He moved closer and I closed my eyes and felt his lips on mine, soft at first and then harder. It was the first time I'd ever been kissed by a boy, and I felt strange and watery inside, like everything was light and floating. I'd wanted to kiss him for a long time. Tyler moved a hand to my face and his fingers traced down my cheek as he kept on kissing me. I felt something so deep inside, I could hardly stand it. I never wanted it to end.

Tyler pulled away. He stood too fast and struggled to catch his balance. His feet managed to find a flat place to stand and he swayed back upright. He took a few careful steps down the first rock before he turned to face me. We looked at each other like we couldn't believe what had just happened. Tyler started to say something then stopped. He took a step backwards. "See you around sometime, Findley. Keep the faith."

He spread his fingers in the *v* of a peace sign. His grin was wide, his eyes dark and shiny. He grinned at me until I smiled.

"See you around sometime, Livingstone."

"I'll write."

"And I'll write back."

I watched him walk away from me for the last time that summer evening as the sun cast last shimmers of golden light across the water. I sat on my rock until long after the mosquitoes and blackflies had come and gone and the beach was hidden by darkness, not knowing if I'd be able to stand another winter waiting to see Tyler Livingstone again. It was a lot of months to spend wondering if his kiss meant anything. It was a long time to miss somebody. I grabbed my book and stood up. It was time to find my mother.

I walked across the beach and then down the road without knowing how I got there. I was torn between this great feeling bubbling up inside of me because of Tyler's kiss and fear that my mother would come home changed somehow. With each step, I promised myself that I would help out more around the store if Mom would just come home and things would go back to the way they used to be. I would be a better daughter and make my father happy. I'd spend time with Elizabeth.

As I started up the path to our store, I hoped against hope that my mother would be back. Still, it was a shock to actually see her sitting on the front steps looking down the path, dressed in her good blue pantsuit and silk blouse that she must have put on for her trip. She jumped up when she saw it was me and crossed the short distance between us. She'd had her hair cut in Toronto and she smelled like Chanel Number Five.

"Where have you been, Darlene? Elizabeth said she hadn't seen you all evening and I was worried."

"I was just watching the sunset at the beach. You didn't need to worry."

She took my arm and hugged me tight. "It's good to be home," she said before letting me go.

"How was your trip?"

"Fine. It was fine. Let's sit for a few minutes."

Relief swung back to fear. This could be the moment that she was going to tell me she was in love with Johnny. I was desperate to hear but scared to know.

"Okay," I said and slowly lowered myself next to her.

"Gideon tells me you've been helping him with some stories. He says you have talent."

I raised my head and stared at her. "When were you talking to Gideon?"

"Earlier. He's hoping you'll see him tomorrow."

"I was going to help you in the store." I remembered the pact I'd made with myself if she came home. I owed her a day of work, even if she didn't know it.

"I'll be fine tomorrow. Your dad will be coming late

in the afternoon and William plans to be here Saturday morning."

"William is still coming? Did you see him in Toronto?"

"I spoke to him on the phone. He has a few things to take care of in Cedar Lake before he heads back to Toronto on Sunday morning."

"That's odd," I said. "What does he need to do in Cedar Lake?"

"Nothing too earth-shattering." Mom stood up and smoothed out the wrinkles in her pants. She shrugged. "I'd like to stay and talk longer but I'm suddenly exhausted. It's been a long day. Thanks again for watching the store today."

"Any time, Mom."

She looked down at me. Her eyes were sad. "I'm sorry I was so critical yesterday. Sometimes I just worry about how you're going to make it through this world with your head always in the clouds. Your father worries too."

"He wants me to be a secretary and get married. What kind of life is that?"

"He … we just want you to be safe and happy." Mom lowered herself to sit next to me again. "He wants all of us to be safe."

I looked straight ahead. "You both just want me to live a life with no risk. I know Annie meant everything to you and I'm sorry she died, but I'm not Annie. You can't keep me in a bubble because you're scared something will happen to me too."

"I didn't think … we never meant to do that, Darlene."

"Then why am I not allowed to do anything or go anywhere?"

"That's not true. We've given you a lot of freedom."

"And we're always worried about what Dad will think or how he'll react. It's like living with an invalid." I didn't care that my mother was sitting stock still beside me, her hands clenched in her lap. I couldn't stop my thoughts from spilling out of my mouth. "We walk around like Annie's death never happened and yet it's everywhere. Every time I go to the beach or sit down for dinner or see the empty chair at the dinner table that would have been hers or look at Dad and know how much he blames me for what happened, I think of Annie. I miss her so much. I'd give anything to have her back, but I can't keep living like there's danger around every corner just waiting to get me. It's … suffocating."

Mom looked at me. Her eyes were shiny. "I had no idea you felt this way. I know it hasn't been easy, but you always seemed even and solid. You were so young when it happened and your father was devastated, completely devastated, but he didn't blame you. We never blamed you. I have no idea where you got that impression."

"Then why does he act like he blames me?"

Her eyes wouldn't let mine go. "Your father blames himself, Darlene. Only himself, and it broke him in ways even I cannot explain. Annie's death made him fearful and fear has made him angry. I have no other explanation. You and William are our world. *You* are my world."

She reached her arms around me and I leaned into her. She ran her hand through my hair like she did when I was little, back and forth in gentle strokes. "Maybe sometimes we assume things. We just get wrapped up in our problems and don't notice the impact we have. I'm sorry, Darlene. I should have realized …" She stopped and I listened to her heart beating against my ear, like comfort and home. Her arms loosened. "I have to get some sleep. We'll talk about this more tomorrow when I can think straight. I really am very tired. Are you going to be okay?"

I nodded into her shoulder and then pulled away. "I'm okay, Mom. Just tired too."

"Then let's both get a good night's sleep and start fresh tomorrow when the sun comes up and our problems don't seem quite so heavy."

Chapter Thirteen

"I'M GOING FOR a bike ride," I said to Elizabeth. I didn't expect her to answer.

It was eleven o'clock and already stifling hot. I'd gotten up early to type my article. I'd wandered downstairs when I was done, and Mom had sent me outside to keep Elizabeth company. Elizabeth hadn't even acknowledged my presence. I was getting bored watching her read another paperback. She was lying in the hammock and I was sitting on the grass nearby. I was sure my mother hadn't meant me to stick around my cousin all day. That would have been cruel.

"It's too hot to bike. We could go for a swim later." Elizabeth glanced up from the Harlequin romance she was reading. The cover had a pirate holding a woman in a low-cut scarlet dress around the waist. She'd borrowed the book from the rack in our store. Her fingers spun a long strand of hair around and around as she read.

"Okay. I'll be back in a few hours, if Mom asks. You and I can go swimming then."

Elizabeth had barely spoken to me since missing the ride to Toronto. I hadn't minded, but I was okay with returning to our truce. I'd gotten used to having her around, even if she was boy crazy and hard to take most of the time. We'd become bonded by our dysfunctional families in some silent, unexplainable kind of way.

I caught glimpses of the bay as I biked down the road toward Gideon's. The water was sparkling as if somebody had dumped a bucketful of diamonds on the surface. It was hypnotic. I rounded a bend while still staring out over the water, and my bike hit a pothole. The front tire wobbled as if my bike was drunk while I struggled to regain my balance. The handle bars twisted in my hands. I dropped a foot to the ground and managed to stop the bike from hitting the pavement. It banged hard against my leg and scratched the inside of my knee. I licked my finger and wiped off the smear of blood before getting back on my bike and pedalling more slowly towards Gideon's.

I found him sitting on the bench in the back garden, snoozing in the sun. A newspaper had fallen to his lap and the pages ruffled in the breeze. Ruby looked up at me from where she lay at his feet, and her tail thumped hard on the ground. I scratched her behind the ears before I sat next to Gideon. He had his head back and was snoring softly. Ruby stood and nuzzled her nose against his leg until he stirred back to consciousness. It took him a few seconds to focus in on me. He grimaced before his jaw went slack.

"Ah, Little Fin. I was hoping you'd stop by today."

"I've finished the first draft of the magazine article. I have notes from my interview with Johnny, but I didn't get too much out of him. Are you feeling okay, Gideon?"

Gideon nodded. "Right as rain. I was hoping you'd find those documents Candy was going to give me. Sounds like you didn't find them."

"No. I didn't have much time to look though."

I handed him my notebook, opened to the right page, and he quickly read through my notes. I waited impatiently.

"You're right. He didn't give you much." Gideon lowered his head and read through the material more closely.

"What did you expect Johnny to tell me?"

Gideon straightened up against the back of the bench. His eyes sharpened. "I wanted him to talk more about the war."

"He said he doesn't like to think about it."

"I'll bet. Did he say when Candy would be back?"

"No, but I know that she wasn't happy here. She told me she might just leave one day."

Gideon's eyebrows shot up. He glanced at my face then looked away. "I wouldn't be surprised. She's a flower child all right, not bound by convention or social mores." Gideon's voice was hoarse. He stopped to breathe between sentences.

"How are you really feeling today? Is your bronchitis really getting better?"

"I'm doing as well as one could ask. I have no complaints. It just takes time." He gathered the newspapers on his lap and set them on the bench in a neat stack. "Let's go in and I'll have a look at your article and make some tea. Get up there, Ruby girl. Out from under my feet."

In the kitchen, I set about boiling water in the kettle while Gideon read my article about summers at Cedar Lake. When I finally set a cup next to him, I could see red markings on my pages and I leaned into him. "Not very good?" I asked. I should never have shown it to him.

"Not bad. Not bad," Gideon muttered. "Just a few structural revisions and it should come together."

He looked at me over his reading glasses as I walked over to the couch and sipped from my mug. The hot tea scalded the roof of my mouth and I put the cup on the coffee table to cool. "If you don't like my writing, you can change it," I said. I folded my arms across my chest and stared down at the table.

"It's a decent first attempt. Better than decent. Don't be too hard on yourself."

"It's just all that red on my page. I worked so hard on every word."

"And it shows, but you have to allow for editorial input. After all, I have a lot more experience than you and have a few tricks of the trade to impart. Being a good writer means taking criticism and being willing to edit. Editing is key." He stood up and reached over to pat my hand. "Your work really has potential. You are a good writer. Good beyond your years. Trust me on this one, Little Fin."

I nodded at his back as he returned to his chair. "Okay," I said. I sat down too and picked up my cup. I held it to my face and blew on the steam. "You talked to my mother yesterday. She told me all about it."

"We had a nice drive to Toronto. It was kind of her to take me."

I smiled. *Mom had gone with Gideon, not Johnny. I was crazy to doubt her.* "Everything went okay then?"

"Well as could be expected. She wanted to visit her sister." Gideon sucked in his breath and looked hard at me. His face was an ashy grey. "They're both worried about Elizabeth."

"Elizabeth?"

"You told me that she came here for the summer to remove her from temptations in Toronto."

"She seems to be doing okay. I don't think this summer will change her, though."

"Probably not, but she'll find her way if given time and support." His eyes studied my face. "Your mother talked quite a bit about your sister Annie. It was the first time she told me about the accident. She said that this summer has had her reliving Annie's loss. She thought it might be because Annie would be the same age as Elizabeth."

I banged my leg against the coffee table. Tea slopped in a milky stain across the wood.

"Are you okay, Darlene? I didn't mean to upset you."

"I'm fine."

Gideon nodded slowly. "I lost my brother too. He was sixteen and at that invincible stage. Wayne was six years older than me and my hero, but his death was not even close to heroic. He was speeding and drove his car into a telephone pole."

"I'm sorry." I was thinking how Mom had hidden her sadness from me. She'd talked to Gideon about Annie instead of to me.

"It was a long time ago, but feels like yesterday sometimes. I still picture Wayne like he was then. That's the thing about someone dying young. They never age in your memory. For a long time, I felt guilty about him dying, as if I could have stopped it from happening. You know, there are still times I have to remind myself that it wasn't my fault. You see, deep down I know that if I hadn't asked him for a ride home that day, he wouldn't have been in his car. He was on his way to get me when it happened."

I looked out the window, away from Gideon's searching eyes.

"But I didn't make my brother drive so fast around that corner. I know now that I had no control over what happened. It took me a long time to forgive myself, but Wayne wouldn't have wanted me to carry it. He wouldn't have wanted that at all."

I made some kind of noise in my throat then set my cup on the coffee table again. "I promised Elizabeth I'd be back soon. I shouldn't keep her waiting."

"Okay, Little Fin." Gideon's voice was gentle. "Come again soon. We need to discuss how we're going to get Johnny to talk about the war."

"Do you think he will?"

"I'll think about the best way to proceed. All people talk if you're patient enough. Sharing what you're feeling can be hard, but I've found it usually makes a person feel better if they get what's bothering them off their chest. It can put things into perspective and give some peace of mind."

My mother was in the store, kneeling on the floor stocking shelves with cans of soup. She looked up and smiled at me.

"There you are, Darlene. Perhaps you could get the box of brown beans from the back and start working in the row next to me. For some reason, baked beans are going like hotcakes this summer."

I looked her over carefully. She had dark circles under her eyes and her hair was damp with sweat. I went to get the beans then kneeled next to her on the floor. We worked silently for a bit, the only sound the cans sliding into place. Finally, she put her hands on the shelf and pushed herself to her feet.

"Well, that ought to do it for now. How about a soft drink? It's one hot day."

"Okay, Mom."

I followed her to the cooler and reached in for a Dr. Pepper. We decided to take our drinks to the front steps. Mom rubbed a cold can of root beer across her forehead and sighed.

"I think the summers are getting hotter. It's odd to actually look forward to autumn."

"Gideon told me that you took him to Toronto yesterday."

"Uh-huh."

"We're working on a few stories together. Did you know Johnny was in the Vietnam War?"

Mom lowered the can of root beer to her lap. Her voice came out too light. "I knew that. I thought you weren't going to be hanging around those people."

"Candy left for Toronto a few days ago too, so I might not get the chance anymore."

"She strikes me as a free spirit."

"I think Johnny's getting ready to leave too."

Mom went very still. "Did he say that to you?"

"No, not exactly." I thought of Tyler. "Too many people are leaving. I wish it could stay summer at Cedar Lake forever. It would be good if we could stop time. I'd even go back a few years."

Back before Annie died.

"You have the same wish as everybody else." Mom stood up and pulled me to my feet. "Go drag Elizabeth away from her silly book and cool off in the lake. I'll start getting supper ready. Your father should be here late afternoon and William tomorrow. We'll have a good weekend together, trying to stay cool in the dog days of summer." She turned with her foot on the top step, her eyes squinting into the bright sunlight. "Promise me you won't bring up Candy and Johnny to your father. It just upsets him. He doesn't like outsiders, especially ones so different."

I made a cross over my heart. "Promise," I said. It was the same promise I'd been making since Annie died. Since they'd taken Dad away to the hospital.

~••~

"Maybe your mother should leave your father," said Elizabeth, squinting through the cigarette smoke as she flicked the ash on the sand between her feet. "She and Johnny would be a better match."

We were sitting next to each other, staring out across the blue expanse of water that was as still as a sheet of paper. I shivered under my towel. We'd had a swim and the water on my skin was giving me goose bumps, even though the air was scorching. "My mother won't leave," I said. I wondered how much Elizabeth knew. She must have seen them together and was fishing for dirt.

Elizabeth turned sideways and looked at me. She slapped me lightly on the leg. "You are so naive." Her laugh tinkled like one of those movie stars in an old Hollywood movie. She opened a bottle of baby oil and started spreading it on her stomach in a slow circular motion. "Johnny and Candy are done. Anybody can see that. Your father is crazy and controlling. It doesn't take a rocket scientist to know where this should lead. The two good-looking sane people are going to be attracted to each other. Johnny and your mother, if I have to spell it out for you. What I can't figure is why your sane, good-looking brother is going for his crazy castoff Candy."

"You're the one who's crazy," I said.

"Your dad will never let your mom go without a fight. He'll go ballistic when your mother leaves him."

"She's not going to leave him."

"I wouldn't be so sure. They married young and she's changed. Your father's trying to keep her on a leash. That's why he gets so angry."

"Since when did you become a family shrink?"

"Like I said, it doesn't take a genius."

I stood and glared down at her. "My mother isn't like that. She's not going anywhere, so I'd appreciate it if you stopped talking like an idiot."

Elizabeth shrugged. She squirted oil onto her leg and let it run down both sides of her thigh onto the towel. "Suit yourself. Don't say I didn't warn you."

"You're an ass sometimes, you know that, Elizabeth? You haven't got a sweet clue what my family is all about." I bit my bottom lip to keep myself from bursting into tears, turned and stomped through the hot sand as fast as I could to get away from her, not caring that my feet were burning with every step.

"And you need to wake up and face reality!" Elizabeth yelled.

Her words followed me to the road, like bad karma. When I reached the end of the sand, I turned around to face her and stuck my middle finger in the air. "Take that," I said, knowing she couldn't hear, even if she hadn't already stretched out on her towel to bake in the sun. "Just go back to Toronto where you belong and leave me and my family alone."

My father still hadn't arrived when Mom finally called me and Elizabeth to the table. She'd let the potatoes and chicken cook too long and it was an effort to swallow the dried out food while my mother chewed hers without seeming to notice. She kept looking towards the doorway to the shop as if she was expecting my father to walk through any second. Elizabeth didn't even hide scraping most of her meal into the garbage pail, and that worried me more than anything. It wasn't like my mother to let us leave the table without finishing our meal.

Dad called at quarter to seven to say that he had to work overtime at the mill and wouldn't make it before Saturday afternoon. Mom's eyes shone with something that looked a lot like relief where she stood holding the phone to her ear. Elizabeth glanced from my mother to me and smiled.

"I'll clean up the dishes, Mom," I said, scooping our dirty dinner plates into a pile.

"I'll be back in a minute to help," said Elizabeth. She grabbed the latest romance novel she'd brought to the table from the store's display rack and headed for the stairs.

Mom smiled at me. "I'll just finish up in the shop then. Maybe I'll close a bit early tonight. I think everyone in Cedar Lake has been by already today."

She left the kitchen humming a song I couldn't place. I turned and started stacking up plates and carrying them to the counter. I was just starting to fill up the sink with soapy water when the phone rang. I picked it up.

"Hello. Oh hi, Aunt Peg. No, I'll get her for you." I set the phone down and called upstairs.

It took Elizabeth a few minutes to clomp down the stairs. She picked up the receiver where I'd left it on the counter, then turned her back on me. "Yeah, Mom?"

I kept running water into the sink, pretending I couldn't hear Elizabeth's side of the conversation when I could hear every word.

"Please stop crying," she said. "You know he always says that. Why do you let him get to you? Stop crying, Mom, and go to bed."

I scraped plates and let the water run so that soap bubbles almost overflowed the sink. I tried not to hear any more. At last, Elizabeth slammed down the receiver and stomped past me without looking. I thought about going after her, but what would I say? It wasn't like she'd ever wanted my sympathy before. I started washing plates instead. The roasting pan proved a greasy challenge, so I slipped it into the sink to soak for a few minutes while I read the paper.

Hunched over the entertainment section, I heard the front door jangle as someone entered the store. My mother's voice mixed with a man's. I raised my head and tried to figure out who had come in.

I crossed the floor to the doorway as quietly as I could, then slipped into the shop and stood behind the last row of Kleenex boxes, paper towels, and toilet paper before moving behind a roll of paper towels so that I could peek out and see the man's profile. I knew before I saw him who it was: Johnny Lewis, standing near the door. He moved out of my range of vision on his way toward the counter, where my mom was sitting on the stool behind the cash. Even from this distance, I knew he'd come for more than a carton of milk. I stuck my head around the corner, but they were still out of sight.

I silently shifted packages of paper towels onto the floor before I sidled forward and angled myself to see in the direction of the counter, but my view was blocked by rows of canned food.

"You really have to leave soon." *My mother's voice.*

"I was hoping you'd changed your mind."

"I never ... you can't believe that was ever a possibility."

"He doesn't appreciate ..." Johnny's voice trailed away, but I could still make out the intensity in the murmur of his words.

"You have to go before they figure it out. You know it's not safe for you here anymore."

"I only stayed this long because I was hoping you'd come with me."

Their voices dropped away. I could hear my mother talking, but I couldn't make out what she was saying, how she answered him. I moved closer to the end of the aisle and tried to see around the end without being seen. By the time I had myself positioned, Johnny had moved behind the counter. I watched him cross the distance to my mother with his arms open.

I took a step forward.

Johnny pulled my mother to her feet and I hesitated, caught between wanting to run to my mother and not wanting her to know I was there. Johnny wrapped his arms around her and she folded into him, like she belonged.

I staggered back and knocked against the metal end of the shelving unit. My hand reached out to steady the shelves before something crashed onto the floor and gave me away. I couldn't take my eyes off them. They were standing locked together, her head resting on his chest and his hand stroking her hair. I wanted to run from my hiding place and pull her from him, but even in my panic, I knew she would never forgive me. Instead, I turned and slipped back into the kitchen. I crossed the floor as quietly as I could, opened the back door, skirted around the side of the house and fled down the path into the woods.

Chapter Fourteen

WHEN I WALKED through the back door into the kitchen an hour later, the lights in the store had been turned off and my mother was gone. I looked around inside, trying to think what I should do about it. My stomach tightened like I was going to throw up. I needed something to take my mind off seeing my mother and Johnny together. Anybody would do.

I raced upstairs in search of Elizabeth, frantically calling her name as I went, and following the music of her pocket radio to the closed door of the bathroom. I knocked hard against the door, resting my head against the wood and called, "Elizabeth, what are you doing tonight?" I pressed both my palms against the door jambs while the smell of strawberry bubble bath and cigarette tobacco spread up from my feet through the gap in the door. I heard splashing, like Elizabeth was flipping over in the water.

Her voice was muffled through the door. "I'm going out with Danny and Michelle. Danny came by when you were out. You can come too if you want."

"Thanks, I will." I ran into the bedroom and stepped out of my clothes, throwing them against the wall. I yanked on a flowered smock top and clean cut-offs. Then I stood in front of the rippled mirror and brushed my hair so fiercely, it crackled like red fire in the last golden sunlight angling across the floor from the open window. My eyes were wild in the glass and my cheeks flaming. I rubbed a hand across my face. Elizabeth must never suspect. She would twist everything I'd seen between Johnny and my mother into an even uglier knot if she knew.

Footsteps squished across the landing. I turned as Elizabeth kicked the door open and strutted in, dropping her towel into a heap by the bed and stretching naked in front of me. Her blonde hair cascaded down her arched back and she smiled at me, her smile sly and mocking at the same time. "You look like the heat is getting to you," she said as she bent to reach for her nylon panties lying on the bed. She shrugged into them and then pulled a T-shirt over her head. It was pink and white with a black peace sign tie-dyed across the front. Her hair left long, splotches of dampness on the fabric as she moved. "We're meeting at Minnow Beach in ten minutes. Danny has beer." She grinned at me out of the side of her mouth then covered her mouth with her hand and pretended to throw up. "I know how much you like beer."

I'd been thinking of asking Elizabeth about how her mother was doing, but not anymore. "Real funny, Elizabeth. I'll wait for you downstairs."

"I'll be down in two secs. Hopefully your thirst will wait that long."

"I'll try to keep myself from drinking the rubbing alcohol."

"Oh, Dar?"

"Yeah?" I turned to face her. She'd turned on the desk lamp and her face was shadowy in the soft light.

"There's not much point you pining after that Livingstone boy any longer. I hear he's leaving Monday. He and Danny are going to Calgary."

"I know. Tyler told me." I spoke like I knew, but I had no idea Danny was going too. I watched a moment longer, trying to figure out what she was up to.

Elizabeth ignored me. She studied herself in my mirror and brushed her long blonde hair while singing along to Frankie Valli and the Four Seasons on her little pocket radio. "You're just too good to be true," she sang, meeting my eyes in the glass. "Funny how guys turn tail and run when they know someone's interested in them." She looked back at her reflection and smiled like she'd gotten the better of me one more time. Like she wasn't at all upset about her mother phoning and crying in her ear.

Danny and Michelle didn't get up from the log they were sitting on when Elizabeth and I crossed the beach to stand in front of them.

"Hey," said Danny to both of us.

Michelle nodded in my direction. She avoided looking at Elizabeth. They'd lit a fire and Michelle's face was puffy in the firelight. When I sat next to her, I could see that she'd been crying. I reached over and touched her arm. She didn't say anything but she smiled at me. Danny's voice was too loud and happy, as if he was trying to make us believe he and Michelle had been having a good time before we arrived. He handed each of us a warm beer from a brown bag next to his feet in the sand. I opened mine and took a long swallow.

"Glad you both could make it. I invited Tyler, but he said he had things to do before we leave tomorrow," said Danny.

"Like kiss Jane Ratherford goodbye," said Elizabeth. She was watching me when she said it. I ignored her.

"So you're going to Calgary," I said to Danny. "Did you decide not to go, Michelle?"

Michelle shook her head. "Not this time."

"Tyler and I might make it as far as Vancouver for a few weeks. We'll catch a bus partway and then thumb," said Danny.

"Will you be back in time for school?" I asked.

"Yeah, I promised my parents, otherwise I wouldn't be going."

"You promised me too," said Michelle.

"Yeah, you too, baby," said Danny, grabbing her hand.

Elizabeth yawned loudly and we all turned our eyes toward her. "Has anyone else found this a deadly boring week? I swear I can't stand being out in the middle of nowhere much longer."

Michelle started to say something, but Danny talked over her. "So how long will be you be staying before you close up for the summer?" He turned to me as he spoke.

"End of August."

"I'll be out of my mind by then," said Elizabeth. "I might have to take up a hobby. I hear skinny dipping is big around here."

"That would be right up your alley," said Michelle.
Elizabeth laughed.

"Has anyone seen Candy around?" I asked.

"My mother said she heard Candy won't be back. She called Johnny yesterday to say she was staying in the city," said Danny.

"You must have the best information network in Cedar Lake," I said. "I live here and I don't hear the half of what you do."

"It's his mother," said Michelle. "She spends her day on the phone milking people for information. I swear the woman's a gossip addict."

"Hey, hey," said Danny. "She's just got a healthy interest in people. She *cares*."

"If that's what you want to call it," said Michelle. She moved closer to Danny until their shoulders were touching.

"She could open up a detective agency," I said.

"That would just validate her obsession," said Danny. "Please, never suggest that within a mile of her spy network."

I wondered if Candy had left because she knew Johnny had something going with my mother. Thinking of her made me feel sick. I drained the beer bottle and set it down next to the log. "I think I'll head home. I hope you have a great trip, Danny. See you next summer."

"I'll send you a postcard," said Danny. He stood up and gave me a hug.

Elizabeth stared at Danny like she was looking right through him. "I'll go back with you, Dar, and leave these two lovebirds alone on their last day together."

"It won't be our last," said Michelle from where she sat on the log. "That's where you've got it wrong."

When we got back to the cottage, my brother's Volkswagen was in the driveway. Elizabeth scooted past me up the back steps and into the kitchen. She was already sitting across from William at the table when I walked in. I leaned against the counter and let myself relax. Mom was in the chair next to William. They each had a hand wrapped around a beer bottle, and I could tell they'd had their heads close together and had been deep in discussion. She leaned back in her seat and raised her eyes to mine. Her face looked tired.

"Candy's decided to stay in Toronto," Elizabeth was saying as I tuned into her chatter. "You wouldn't have something to do with that, would you?"

"Not me." William's eyes locked on mine. "Looks like Candy just decided it was time to move on."

"It's all pretty peculiar," I said. "She and Johnny seemed close. She wanted it to work out between them."

Elizabeth laughed, her eyes on my brother. "You're so young, little cousin. You have no idea how women like Candy operate."

William shifted in his chair and took a drink from the beer bottle. My mother frowned at Elizabeth.

"It's wrong to break up a couple that's trying to make their relationship work," I insisted. "Married couples should stay together. Especially if they have children."

"Do you want to go for a walk, Darlene?" William asked a little too quickly. He looked at Mom and she nodded, a movement so slight, I wouldn't have noticed if I hadn't glanced her way. Elizabeth went to jump in and invite herself along, but Mom got there first.

"I need you to come upstairs and help me for a minute, Elizabeth," Mom said. "Let's go now before I get ready for bed."

Elizabeth opened her mouth and looked as if she was about to refuse, but we all stood and William turned his back on her, motioning for me to follow.

We didn't talk until we'd crossed the beach and started climbing to my lookout. The moon was full and the sand bathed in a whitish light. Waves were lapping on the shore and sliding back into the lake like big slurps. William seemed far away and I didn't know how to begin talking about all the worrisome thoughts going around and around in my head. He turned to look down at me from his toehold in the rock. I could just make out his eyes in the moonlight. He grabbed my hand and pulled me up the last few feet. I settled myself next to him, my arm resting against his.

"I wish this summer had never happened," I said. "People are getting weird."

"How so?"

"Mom. She doesn't seem happy anymore." I hesitated. "Do you think she'll ever leave Dad?"

William was quiet for a while. Then he said slowly, "No. I don't. You can't judge what goes on in their relationship, Dar. It's only the two people involved who really know."

"Then how can you say she won't leave him? What if someone else comes along she loves better?"

"Mom is stronger than Dad, no matter how he blusters and acts all in control. She knows what it would do to him if she left."

And to the rest of us.

"I saw you kissing Candy." My confession came out like an accusation. I hadn't meant it to.

William let his breath out in a long sigh and pulled his arm away from mine. "It's complicated. Johnny asked me to help with Candy."

"Help him how?"

"If I tell you this, you'll have to keep it secret. You need to swear."

I thought it over for a split second. "I swear."

"Cross your heart?"

"And hope to die."

William found a stick and began digging it into the rock at his feet. "You know that little war going on in Southeast Asia? Well, some of us believe it's wrong for the U.S. government to be drafting men to send them to kill people in another country for a cause that rests basically on power, corruption, and greed. A war that the Americans shouldn't be fighting. One they can't possibly win."

"I hate the war too, but what's that got to do with anything?"

"Some of the men being conscripted into the U.S. army fled to Canada instead of serving."

"The draft dodgers."

"Yeah, the draft dodgers."

I sat up straighter. "*You're* helping the draft dodgers? Is that what Johnny is?"

"Well, yes and no. I'm part of the network helping them start up new lives in Canada, but Johnny isn't a draft dodger exactly."

"What is he then?"

"Johnny was a pilot in the air force in Nam. He was there five years. Thing is, he went AWOL. That's a bigger deal than running away from the draft."

"You mean he ran out on the air force?"

"Exactly. But it's a little worse than that." William leaned closer. "He saw things that could get people court martialled, and he took some documents when he left. People are desperate to find him. Not to mention, he'll be court martialled for deserting and will get to spend several years in prison. The Americans don't like it when somebody leaves their military without permission."

"If his name is Johnny Lewis, isn't it stupid for him to be using his real name?" William sat silently beside me and I started thinking it through. "But that isn't his real name, is it? And he didn't spend his summers here, and he doesn't really know Mom from when they were kids?"

"We sent Johnny and Candy here with a bit of help from Mom. There was a Lewis family that used to come here in the summers, and they had a son, but I have no idea where the real Johnny Lewis is at this moment."

"So why use his name?"

"People here remember the Lewises, and they wouldn't think twice about Johnny coming back for the summer. Remember, Johnny Lewis was just a little kid the last time they were here. Mom came up with the idea after she found out the Davidsons weren't coming to the lake this summer. She organized the cottage rental."

I kept thinking out loud. "So those men staying with Johnny and Candy were other deserters and that's why they kept out of the way. But what about Candy? Why did she leave?"

"She's fine. We … that is, our network figured we had to get her out of here. She was threatening to talk about things that have to be kept secret … at least, for now."

My mind started scrambling through the possibilities. "She was going to give some documents to Gideon the night of the beach party. That is before you started kissing her." I turned sideways to look at him more closely. "Were you taking one for the team? Distracting her so she agreed to go away?"

William hesitated. "Johnny's got military documents

that could get him killed. We're protecting him so that he can testify when the time is right. Candy was a loose cannon and I am prepared to do whatever is necessary to protect him. For your information, not that it's any of your business, I honestly care for Candy."

"What documents?"

"Johnny was friends with one of the soldiers who tried to stop the massacre in My Lai. There were three of them. They gave statements, first-hand descriptions. There were also memos about how to handle the situation. Johnny was in a position to get copies. The army doesn't want any of this shared with the public."

I chewed my bottom lip as I thought it over. "Why not just let the media print the story?"

"People could be at risk more than they are now. There have been threats, hate mail, and even dead animals placed on the doorsteps of the three who tried to stop the slaughter. It's not time yet."

"What's Johnny's real name?"

"It's better if you don't know. Candy used her real first name but picked a different last name. That's as much as I'm going to say."

"I can't believe you used her like that."

"Sometimes you have to do things you don't want to do for a bigger cause. She ... figured out in Toronto that I'd fallen for her, and she flirted like crazy. I started to spend time with her. It hurt when I figured out that she was just trying to make Johnny jealous. I started keeping my distance."

"Will Johnny stay here much longer?"

"We're moving him tomorrow to another location. I'm here to make it happen. I'll be bringing the last of Candy's things to her in Toronto when I go home afterwards."

"And Mom?"

"She'll know that she's been part of something more important than all of us. Someday, the history books will tell the full story, but for now, I'm counting on your silence."

"You know I won't say anything that could get you or Mom in trouble."

"You can't breathe a word to Dad."

"Cross my heart," I said again. "Dad thinks deserters are scum. No wonder Mom doesn't want him to know."

"Mom's done a lot of good work. You know there's an underground network run out of Toronto? They help the draft dodgers get to Canada and start new lives."

"How did she get involved?"

"One of her visits to Toronto. I told her I was thinking about joining up because I wanted her advice. She said I should and that she was going to join as well. It wasn't long after we found out about My Lai. It got real hard to look away."

"And that's how she met Johnny?"

"Yes. They met in November on one of her visits. Dar, if they keep digging, it could put Mom in jeopardy, and I don't mean just with Dad. I won't let that happen. If it means leading Candy on for now, I can live with it."

"I still don't get why Candy came to Canada if she and Johnny weren't together, you know, as a couple."

"You really don't know? Candy is Sean's mother. She and Johnny were supposed to get married when he came back from Nam, but she started living with somebody else while he was overseas."

"But Sean is Johnny's too right? Otherwise, he wouldn't have taken on him and Candy."

"You just have to look at Sean to know he's Johnny's kid."

"She would leave Sean just like that?"

William's voice got so low, I could hardly hear him. I leaned closer. "… Johnny doesn't love her the way she loves him. I think the baby reminds her of what she'll never have, what she threw away by being unfaithful."

William put his arm around me and I leaned my head on his shoulder. We sat like that for a while, neither of us saying anything, just thinking our own thoughts and listening to the waves slapping onto the beach.

"Just so you know, I don't feel good about any of this," William said. "I just can't see another way out that wouldn't hurt the network … and Mom."

"I know."

We stood up at the same time and started climbing down the rocks, William ahead of me in the darkness. When we reached the sand, I looked out at the silver light on the water. I said a prayer for Annie as I did every night before going inside.

Chapter Fifteen

THE NEXT MORNING, I had breakfast then biked over to Gideon's. I wanted to let him know that Candy was staying in Toronto and he should give up on his Pulitzer Prize idea. He wasn't going to like it. I knew that for sure.

Ruby was waiting to be let in at the back door when I arrived, her nose pressed against the door as if she was trying to push it open. I was surprised to find Gideon making toast, still dressed in his pajamas. Usually, he was up and working at his typewriter by five a.m. Classical music was playing on his little kitchen radio.

"You're up late today," I said as I put the kettle on for tea.

"Just a slow morning. I worked until past midnight on my column for the *Globe* and decided to sleep in as a reward for getting it done."

His eyes were shiny as if he had a fever, his face pale.

"Are you feeling okay?"

"You keep asking me that like a little mother hen. I'm right as rain, child. However, I think it's time for my medicine, so I'll just go change and take my pills, if you would be so kind as to make the tea."

"Aye aye, sir."

I busied myself making the tea then brought the mugs to our usual spots. When Gideon sat down at the typewriter, he'd put on a bulky cable knit sweater and jeans, even though it was another warm morning. He sipped from the cup and swallowed some big white pills while watching me over the rim. Ruby circled the room then plunked herself down at his feet with a big sigh.

"Those look hard to choke down."

"Antibiotics. Good for what ails." Gideon said, setting his mug on the desk. "Any word if Candy's returned?"

"Johnny says she won't be coming back."

Gideon sighed. "I was supposed to meet her that night of the last beach party." His eyes were thoughtful.

"I thought I saw you at the beach. Were you waiting for her there?"

"She was supposed to come to my house, but she never showed up. She'd called me earlier that day and said she had something to give me that would make a huge story. At the time, I thought she sounded like she was angry. Naturally enough, I thought she was mad at that Johnny fellow and ready to give me something I could use in a huge story. I should have known it wouldn't be that easy."

"Is that why you think she left so suddenly?"

"I did find it odd that she caught a bus out of here so fast."

I shifted uncomfortably in my seat. I couldn't say anything without giving away my brother. Gideon had always told me not to say anything to a journalist that you didn't want printed. "There's no 'off the record' when it comes to a story," he'd told me countless times. Gideon was my friend, but he was a journalist above all.

He picked up a piece of paper to end the subject. "Thought you might like to read my latest offering on the war effort."

"Okay."

I got up and took the paper from him, happy that he'd changed the topic of conversation. I stood next to him while I read it, and then set the paper on the desk. I tried not to let on that I was disturbed by the topic. "You've written about draft dodgers. It's a good piece."

He glanced over at me. His eyes were amused. *What did he know about Johnny and William and my mother?* He'd sent me to interview Johnny and had phoned ahead. Whatever he'd said to Johnny had made him talk to me, as if Gideon was holding something over him.

Gideon cleared his throat. "Seems like an issue that needs some coverage. The U.S. government needs to rethink what it's forcing these young men and women to do in the name of patriotism. This could be my best bit of writing in a long time."

"It's strong," I said. "Did you talk to some of the deserters?"

"I met a few dodgers in Toronto over the past few years. They weren't too keen to be interviewed until they were sure I wouldn't be printing names and addresses.

It's not as if I'd do anything to support the war effort. I'm one hundred percent behind people who decide they don't have the stomach to fight."

"Did you find any draft dodgers here at Cedar Lake?"

"You never know where they're hiding out." Gideon was still watching me. His quick smile came and went. "How's your mother?"

"Good."

Gideon stooped down to rub Ruby behind the ears. "That's my lovely old girl," he said as he rubbed his hand across her back. "Did I tell you the story of how I got Ruby?"

"I thought you said somebody gave her to you."

"Not exactly. I was driving here from Toronto one evening. It was a cool October day, if I remember, and I saw something lying by the side of the road. Looked like a bag of garbage at first. I slowed to have a better look and that's when I realized it was a dog lying there. For some reason I couldn't just drive by, even though I thought the animal was dead. I pulled over and when I got out, Ruby here lifted her head and looked me square in the eyes, like she believed I'd been sent to save her."

"What did you do?"

"The only thing I could do. Loaded her into my back seat and took her to the vet in the next town. He set her leg and sewed her up. Luckily, she'd only been dealt a glancing blow from whatever lowlife hit her with their car and left her there to die. I put out the word where the owner could pick her up, but nobody ever tried to claim her. I was glad for that. It would have been tough to give her back."

"It must have been fate that you drove by when you did."

"Turns out Ruby's been my most faithful companion for these eight years, so I was the lucky one."

I finished my tea and stood up. "I guess I'll go back and help Mom in the store. Dad's arriving this morning and William leaves later today."

"You're having a busy time of it. I wonder if you could do me a favour tomorrow."

"Sure. Just name it."

"I have to go into town for the day, so I wonder if you could come by, feed Ruby around lunchtime, and take her for a walk."

"Of course I will. Is the house key in the same flowerpot?"

"Same as always. I'll owe you one."

"I'll put it on your tab."

I turned at the back door to smile back at Gideon. He started to say something but changed his mind and returned my smile with a quick one of his own and a wave. He'd already swung around to start typing as I stepped outside into the bright sunshine. The last picture I had of Gideon before I turned to open the door was him bending down to pat Ruby's upturned head while her tail thump-thumped against the hardwood floor.

I was halfway home and had just passed the split in the road that led to the Davidson cottage. I was torn between rushing home to be near my mother and making one last trip to see Johnny and Sean before they left Cedar Lake for good. What William had told me made me look at Johnny differently. Maybe I wanted him to know.

I started pedalled more slowly. I wasn't feeling too brave about facing Johnny again. Gideon always told me to follow the story, no matter where it led. I guess that also went for stories that were never going to make it into print. I turned the front wheel of my bike toward the Davidsons' and started pedalling for their driveway.

This time Johnny's flowered van was the only vehicle in the laneway. I stretched to look in the windows as I biked by. The back was loaded with boxes and suitcases. I got off my bike and leaned it against a tree just as Johnny came out of the cottage carrying a box of toys. He didn't see me right away, and I took a second to watch him now that I knew he was a man on the run. He was wearing a white T-shirt and his arm muscles were bulging. I hadn't realized how strong he was. A red bandana was tied around his forehead that held the black curls away from his face.

I took a deep breath and stepped forward. Johnny nodded in my direction before setting the box on the floor of the van. He slammed the door and turned to face me. His eyes weren't friendly exactly, but not angry either. He spoke first.

"I guess you've figured out that Sean and I are moving on."

"Where will you go?"

"I'm not sure. Maybe down east ... or out west. Hell, could be up north with the Eskimos. Doesn't really matter anymore. There's nothing keeping us here."

"Will you be seeing Candy?"

Johnny crossed his arms across his chest. "Maybe. Probably not. I figured you of all the people around here would be sorry to see her gone. She seemed to like you."

"Did Candy really know all those famous people she talked about?"

Johnny sighed. "I'm not sure why I'm going to tell you this, but maybe it's just because of all your family's done for me. Come sit for a minute where I can hear Sean if he wakes up. I'm going to feed him and then we're on our way."

I followed Johnny into the kitchen and sat at the table while he pushed himself up onto the counter so that he was looking down at me. The kitchen was spotless, as if nobody had lived there for the summer. The appliances were shiny enough to make even Mrs. Davidson happy. Only Sean's bowl and a jar of baby food were left on the counter.

"Candy," said Johnny as he pulled a cigarette out of a package in his pocket, "in case you didn't know, isn't quite like other people. She grew up down the road from me in South Carolina and was always full of ideas and stories and dreams about going places and being somebody. Her mother left when she was three and her father never had any money. He drove a truck and was gone a lot. She was always getting picked on by the other kids for being dressed badly and for tagging along. I felt sorry for her and tried to look out for her. We got to be friends." He shrugged. "Later, more than friends." He struck a match and inhaled smoke from the cigarette as the end lit bright red. He squinted at me through the smoke as he exhaled.

"So was Frances really Sean's mother like she told me, or is Candy Sean's mother?" I asked.

"Candy told so many stories, I don't think she knew the truth half the time. She was a chronic liar. However, I can tell you that she is Sean's mother. No question about that. She told me I was the father and I've decided to believe it. I was home on leave about the right time."

"Sean looks like you."

"I know, but it doesn't matter if he isn't mine. As far as I'm concerned, he's my kid."

"Why did Candy make up stuff?"

"It was her way of coping, living inside her head and making her world better than what it was." Johnny shrugged. "I know I'm making her sound like a loony tune, but she wasn't. She was just getting by the best she could. Lately though, she'd gotten to be more than I could handle. I didn't feel I could leave her alone with Sean anymore."

"I would have liked to say goodbye."

"Candy isn't much for goodbyes, but don't worry, she won't forget you. She doesn't let go of people easily."

"Why did she come to Canada with you?"

"When I got back from Nam, she told me to take Sean because she didn't think she could look after him. The truth was her new boyfriend didn't like kids. I bunked on their couch the night before I left for the Canadian border. Candy had a big fight with the guy over Sean, and he stormed out. In the morning, Candy convinced me that I'd get across easier with a woman pretending to be my wife. She was right about that."

"She told me that she was crazy about you."

"Maybe that was true once. The long and short of it is that she didn't like to be alone. If I hadn't left when I did for Nam, well, who knows? Anyhow, I knew we wouldn't work out when I got back, but it didn't seem right to leave her behind. There was also Sean to think about. I never let Candy believe we'd be anything more than friends when I let her come to Canada with me, even though it didn't stop her from trying."

I thought about my mother. She was the polar opposite of Candy, and the way Johnny had looked at her made me think about what my mother was giving up staying with us. I shifted uncomfortably in my chair. I could hear Sean stirring in the other room.

Johnny said, "Candy always lands on her feet. Some people have that talent." He took another drag from the cigarette before standing up to get an ashtray from the cupboard. He sat back down.

"Look, Candy was mad at me for rejecting her and she was like a child when she realized she wasn't going to get her way. She was like two different people — warm and giving one minute and spiteful and childish the next. I told her to go back to Toronto, that we were through. Your brother finally convinced her to go the other night. I just couldn't look out for her any more. Sean is my priority now."

"I know." I thought of how she'd left Sean alone in his crib when we went to the beach. I'd known it was wrong.

Johnny looked toward the hallway and the direction of Sean's voice crying out for him, and I stood to leave. Johnny jumped from the counter and landed in front of me. He reached into the back pocket of his jeans. "I think Candy would like you to have this." He held out a silver ring with a dove's head carved into the band. I'd remembered seeing it on the ring finger of her left hand the last time we'd gone swimming.

"She might want it back."

"Candy gives things she cares about to her friends. She likes you."

I reached over, took it from his hand, and slipped it onto my middle finger. The metal was warm from his pocket.

Johnny took a step toward the door, then turned and looked at me. "You know you have a way of looking at people that makes them feel like you're seeing clear through them. Keeps you a little off balance. You get that from your mom." He cleared his throat and looked away. "Well, anyway, give her my best. I hope to see you again sometime."

"Yeah, me too." *But not really.*

I started walking away from him but stopped and turned as I reached the door. "What was it like? You know, being in Vietnam."

Johnny closed his eyes. When he opened them again, he looked past me out the window. "It was the stuff of nightmares. Stifling hot days in the jungle, so humid your clothes were soaking wet even after a shower. The drone of mosquitoes was constant. It filled my dreams. I never slept well, always waking up after a few hours. I used to look forward to my shifts dropping bombs on the Viet Cong. It's an impersonal way to kill people, and I did it well. We were all scared, but some handled it better than others. Then there was the monotony. When you weren't flying, there was nothing to do and nowhere to go. Drugs were easy to get. A lot of the guys started using just to get through. I missed home and the thought of Candy waiting for me kept me going. Toward the end, all I wanted to do was get back to her, to something untouched by what we were doing in Nam." He shrugged. "I was nuts to think she'd be the same as I left her. Five years I was more or less gone. I still wake up in a sweat, thinking I'm back there in the jungle. Hearing sounds in my head that won't go away."

I suddenly wanted to get away from Johnny and what I saw in his eyes. "I hope it goes well for you and Sean," I said. "I hope you find somewhere good to live."

He rubbed a hand across his eyes and nodded. His cheeks were wet. "Yeah, you take care."

Johnny was already halfway up the stairs to get Sean when I shut the back door. I stepped outside into the heat of another August day. I could still hear Sean's cries through the open window, then the low murmuring of Johnny's voice followed by silence. I stepped onto the pathway and walked past the bench where Candy and I had sat talking in the sun not very long ago, trying to picture her there, but already finding her features were fading in my memory. I glanced back one more time as I straddled my bike seat and prepared to push off from the grass with one foot.

Chapter Sixteen

MY FATHER'S RUSTY blue Ford was next to William's Volkswagen in our driveway. I walked my bike slowly past them up the drive. Dad and William were probably sitting at the kitchen table reading the paper while Mom made them something to eat. She'd have poured them each a strong cup of coffee in her good china mugs and sat for a minute before getting up to keep busy at the counter. She'd be pretending that it was just another Saturday morning and she wasn't distracted by Johnny's leaving. She wouldn't let on that she was part of the network helping him move. William would be acting right along with her.

I looked across the road toward the lake. I thought about going to go sit on my rock and being alone. Nobody would miss me for a little bit. After they ate lunch, Mom would probably start looking at the clock and asking if anyone had seen me. She'd go to the front door and look up the road. She wouldn't rest until I came home. I looked back toward the store and sighed.

I didn't want my mom to have to worry about me. I'd go sit on my rock after I had something to eat.

"There you are," said my father. He looked up from his plate of fried eggs and bacon. Pockets of flesh sagged under his eyes, but he didn't look as tired as he had every other time I'd seen him at Cedar Lake. This morning he nodded at me. "You're looking tanned."

I stopped myself from turning my head to look behind me to see if he was talking to somebody else. Had he actually noticed me and not told me I was doing something wrong? "Hi, Dad. Hard week?"

"I've had better."

William and Mom locked eyes before Mom looked at me and shook her head to warn me not to talk about anything going on behind the scenes. I kept my eyes on her.

"Where's Elizabeth?"

"Babysitting. Apparently she's quite a hit with the kids," said my mother.

"That girl will go far in life," said my father. "She's got spunk." He bit into a piece of toast.

My mouth fell open. William grinned at me before standing up from the table. "Well, I hate to leave so soon, but I have to head back to Toronto," he said.

"You're always in a hurry," Dad said. "Where's the fire this time?"

"Some unexpected volunteer work."

"I'll walk out with you," I said.

When we stopped halfway down the steps, William said, "Thanks for keeping all this Johnny business a secret from Dad. I'm off to get Johnny now. We've got a new location where he and Sean can stay for a while."

"I think you're doing a good thing, you and Mom," I said.

"I'm glad you're onside." William smiled before he looked down at my hand. His voice came out strange. "Where did you get that ring?"

I looked down too and held my hand out in front of me. "Johnny gave it to me. He said Candy would want me to have it."

William grabbed my hand and touched the ring with one of his fingers.

"What's wrong?" I asked.

"Nothing. It's nothing." He pulled back his hand, and we kept walking toward his car. He opened the driver's door and put one foot inside before turning back to look at me. "Oh, by the way, you might also want to watch how much personal information you tell Elizabeth. She seems to know a lot about you, actually. More than I thought you'd ever share."

"What do you mean?"

"Just that she told us at the campfire about your crush."

My face felt hot. "Who did Elizabeth tell?"

"Everyone standing around … including Tyler."

I nodded but couldn't say anything. This was worse than when my tights had fallen down in grade three while I was demonstrating my new etch-a-sketch for show and tell.

William said, "I don't think she got the reaction she wanted."

"What do you mean?"

"Tyler. He didn't say anything. He just stood there looking at her. Then he put his head down and his hands in his pockets and walked away. He never looked back at anybody or said goodbye. I just thought you should know."

"Thanks."

"Any time." William reached over and squeezed my arm.

After he'd driven away, I raced back inside and up the stairs to my bedroom. I reached under the bed for my diary and saw that it was still locked. I crossed to my jewellery box and found the key on top of the piece of leather I wore around my neck. I always tucked the key underneath and out of sight. There was no doubt in my mind that Elizabeth had been in my things.

I dropped to my knees on the floor and worked the lock open. The pages fell open. I flipped to the last two pages and skimmed through the entries that recorded my pain at seeing Tyler with Jane Ratherford and my fear that he was interested in my cousin. That must have given Elizabeth a laugh. She'd read my most personal thoughts and then used them to humiliate me. Hot, angry tears leaked from my eyes. If the floor had opened up at that moment, I'd have gladly dropped through it into another dimension that didn't include my cousin or Tyler Livingstone.

~••~

Michelle and I spent the afternoon at the beach. We didn't say much, just swam and tanned. Neither of us wanted to talk about Danny and Tyler and how Elizabeth had played us all summer. Michelle flipped from her back onto her stomach next to me on her towel. She propped herself up on her elbows.

"I guess Danny and Tyler are half-way to Sault Ste. Marie." She turned her head sideways and looked at me, waiting.

"I know about Elizabeth telling everyone that I like Tyler," I said as if it was the most boring piece of news in the universe.

Michelle sat up quickly. "I didn't want to say anything. I couldn't believe it when she told him and everyone at the beach."

"Well, that's my cousin. Treats everyone equally badly."

"I don't know how you can stand her."

"It's just for a few more weeks and then I hope to never spend time with her again. What about you and Danny?"

"I don't know. He thinks we're fine, but I'm not sure about him anymore, you know?"

"Yeah, I know."

"I'm going to the Maritimes with my parents for a holiday," said Michelle suddenly. "I'm not coming back here again this summer."

"It'll be good to have a break before school."

"My mother has a sister in Halifax, and I'm thinking about applying there for university next year."

"Will Danny be going with you?"

"I haven't told him where I'm applying. I probably won't." Michelle looked out across the lake and sighed. "Maybe your cousin Elizabeth did me a favour. I mean, if that's all it took for Danny to fool around on me, it wasn't going to last, you know?"

"I guess."

"I know. You're lucky that you never got in deep with Tyler. He's a lot like Danny."

I nodded, but I didn't believe it, because sometime between William telling me what Elizabeth had done and sitting in the sand with Michelle, I'd remembered Tyler's kiss on my mouth. His kiss had felt like a promise. It had felt right. I'd remembered how he'd looked at me afterwards, standing above me on the edge of the rock, his eyes surprised but all lit up inside. He hadn't been making fun of me as Elizabeth had hoped. Sitting in the sand next to Michelle, I'd stopped feeling bad about Elizabeth's treachery because it didn't matter. If anything, her letting Tyler know that I liked him had probably helped. She'd told him and he'd come to wait for me on my rock. He'd kissed me, knowing how I felt about him. I might not have all Elizabeth's dating rules down pat, but I knew enough to recognize a good sign when I saw it.

Elizabeth spent the evening at another babysitting job. I pretended to be asleep when she came up to bed after eleven. I was done with her. I didn't care anymore that she was part of my family with a screwed-up life. She'd violated my privacy and I couldn't forgive her. She clumped around the room, dropping her shoes onto the floor and made enough noise to wake me if I'd been truly asleep, but I kept my breathing deep and regular and did fall asleep after she left to go to the bathroom.

I managed to get up before her and spent the day helping in the store, winning my father's approval and keeping away from Elizabeth. Only a few more weeks and she'd be gone and I wouldn't have to look at her anymore.

At four o'clock, I remembered my promise to Gideon. I'd forgotten all about taking Ruby for a walk and she'd be clawing at the door to get outside. Dad was behind the counter ringing in money from some kids who were buying chocolate bars. I waited impatiently for them to finish.

"Is it okay if I leave for an hour? I have to go let Gideon's dog out."

Dad looked around. His eyes were puzzled. "Have you seen your mother lately? She's been gone for some time."

"I think she went upstairs to lie down."

Dad frowned. "That's not like your mother. She never naps in the afternoon."

I started toward the door. "I won't be long, Dad. I'll watch the store when I get back."

"Okay," Dad said. He was walking toward the kitchen but stopped and looked at me. "Better take your jacket. Radio says a storm's moving in. If you get caught at Gideon's in a downpour, give me a call and I'll come get you."

"Is your headache gone?" I asked.

"For the time being." He rubbed a hand across his forehead. His voice was gruff. "I took you mother's advice and saw the doctor in Ottawa. He's given me some new medication." It was as close to an apology as Dad would ever give — an admission he'd been unwell.

"I'm glad," I said.

Dad nodded. "Don't forget to call if you need a lift home. I don't like the look of those clouds."

"I'll be okay, but thanks, Dad." I stopped at the door with my hand on the knob. When I looked back, he'd gone into the kitchen. He was sitting down at the table to read the paper. He glanced up and nodded at me. I felt something loosen in my chest as I pulled open the door to step outside. The knot didn't feel as tight.

I should have run back for my windbreaker but didn't want to waste any more time. I raced outside and had to hold onto the door to keep it from banging shut behind me. I pedalled my bike as fast as I could against the gusty wind. Low, dark clouds had gathered and the air had cooled down as it does before a rainstorm. By the time I passed the Davidsons I wished I'd listened to my dad and put something on over my T-shirt. Cold drops of rain had begun to fall and I pedalled harder. If it hadn't been for Ruby, I would have turned around and beat it for home.

By the time I reached his yard, the rain was coming down in a slanting sheet, running into my eyes like a faucet from my dripping hair. It soaked through my clothes until they felt like a second wet skin. Gideon's car was in the driveway. He'd know I hadn't kept my promise to take Ruby outside. I felt bad but good at the same time knowing that Ruby wouldn't be frantic. Nanny's bleats rose above the howling wind that was pushing against my bike and taking my breath away. I walked my bike the last distance up the path and laid it on the wet grass before making a dash for the back door. Gideon didn't answer when I knocked, so I turned the door knob. The door swung open as if the house had been waiting for me.

"Gideon!" I called, but nobody answered. I moved deeper into the entranceway. The house was dark with the rain and wind lashing against the windows. I slipped out of my wet sandals and left them on the mat, then crossed the kitchen in my bare feet on my way to Gideon's office. The coolness of the floor seeped through my skin. The living room was in semi-gloom, but I could still make out Ruby lying on the floor near Gideon's desk. The only sound besides the wind was the clock ticking on the mantelpiece.

"Ruby girl, here I am," I said, bending and clapping my hands for her to come to me. She stood and stretched but flopped back down, letting her head droop onto her front paws. She whined deep in her throat.

"I know. I should have come sooner." I moved around the couch to turn on the lamp on the end table. I turned as I said, "Is Gideon having a nap?" I stopped talking when I looked back toward Ruby, because Gideon wasn't in his bedroom resting at all. He was sitting in his desk chair, facing away from me, his chin tucked against his chest. At first, I thought he was sleeping. I tiptoed closer. He'd been looking tired lately. Maybe I should let him sleep. Still, it was almost suppertime.

"Gideon!" I said more softly. "I'm sorry I'm so late."

Ruby whimpered and pushed her head against Gideon's leg as if she was nudging him to pay attention. I looked closer. He was wearing a maroon housecoat I'd never seen before, frayed around the cuffs and collar, with blue striped pyjamas visible beneath the desk. I felt like an intruder, like I'd caught him with his guard down. He would hate me seeing him like this. I took a step backwards while my mind took in all the details without really registering them — the full cup of tea on the desk, the clock ticking, Gideon's hands folded in his lap, feet in his favourite leather slippers, the unnatural paleness of his skin. I changed direction and moved beside him as if outside my own body.

"Gideon," I called more urgently. I'd begun shivering and couldn't stop. "Wake up, Gideon. I'll make a fresh pot of tea." I reached out my hand. "It's time to wake up." I dropped my hand until it rested on his. It was cold and still and I pulled my hand away. "No," I whispered. I couldn't make myself move. "Gideon, you have to wake up. I'll make some tea."

My parents arrived before the ambulance, which had to come all the way from Campbellford. My mother's voice echoed through the kitchen and down the hallway, calling my name over and over.

"In here," I called.

My mother found me first. Her face was pale and her eyes wet. She crossed the floor and put an arm around my shoulders. Dad was right behind her. He stood back a step, holding onto his baseball cap, turning it around and around in his rough hands. He looked at Gideon and then around the room. Mom squeezed my arm.

"Why don't we wait for the ambulance outside? I called from home and it should be on its way. The rain has almost stopped."

"I think I'll wait here with Gideon. He wouldn't want to be left alone."

I looked down at my hand, holding onto Gideon's. It was strange. I'd never held Gideon's hand when he was alive. Why was I holding onto it now like I had the right?

"We could just go sit on the couch," Mom said. "We could wait there until the ambulance comes."

"Okay," I said but I couldn't let go of Gideon's hand even after Mom tried to pull me away. I hung on tighter if anything. "His hand is cold," I said, "and stiff. Maybe, you could get him a blanket."

"I could do that," said Mom carefully. She let go of me and I could hear her cross the floor to the bedroom. I couldn't take my eyes off Gideon. Ruby whined at his feet and I felt her stir against my legs.

Dad made a noise in his throat. "Gideon looks peaceful, Darlene."

I nodded.

"Here comes your mother with that blanket. We won't leave until the ambulance comes."

"Okay." I nodded again. My head felt as if it was too heavy for my neck.

Mom wrapped the blanket around Gideon's legs. She tucked it around him and looked up at me. Her eyes were trying to tell me something. "I'll make some tea," she said. "We can have a cup while we wait."

I nodded. I could feel tears dripping down my cheeks. They didn't seem part of me. Gideon and I should be drinking tea now and talking about my story.

Dad murmured something to my mother as she slipped past him. I could hear a siren somewhere outside, coming closer up the road. Dad put a hand on my back.

"They're coming now, Darlene. It's time for us to take Ruby home."

I looked down at Ruby's big black head. She had her chin resting on her front paws. "You won't mind if she comes with us?"

"No." Dad moved his hand to cover mine. "No, Ruby can come stay with us. Let go of Gideon's hand now, Darlene. It's time we take Ruby outside. Gideon will be looked after and we'll visit him again tonight if you want. You'll have time to say goodbye."

"Okay, Dad."

I felt his fingers move under mine and then the pressure of his hand pulling my hand from Gideon's. Dad wrapped his other arm around my waist and walked with me to the door where Mom was waiting. "You go with your mother now and I'll bring Ruby outside. Then I'll stay with Gideon until it's time for him to leave. He won't be alone." Dad patted me awkwardly on the back before going back inside.

Chapter Seventeen

Gideon had a sister. Her name was Phyllis Higgins and she lived in Regina, Saskatchewan. She asked me to come see her at Gideon's house after the service in Campbellford on Wednesday morning. Mom sent me over with a Sara Lee white layered cake she'd defrosted for lunch. "You can't go empty-handed," she'd said. I put it in my knapsack, hoping it wouldn't get squashed, and biked over mid-afternoon.

Phyllis was short like Gideon, with the same sharp brown eyes and messy hair. I had liked her right away when I'd first met her at the funeral home.

"Back here!" she called to me, and I followed her voice to the back bedroom. She was sitting cross-legged on the floor, wearing jeans and a loose blue sweater, sorting through the drawers that she'd pulled out from Gideon's dresser. "The man didn't invest much in fashion," she said then gave me the same quick smile as Gideon. She finished folding a pair of pants before pushing herself to her feet. "Tea time, I think."

"I have cake," I said. "It's just a frozen one."

"Cake and tea. Perfect."

We found seats across from each other on the couch. She saw me looking at Gideon's empty desk.

"I've been packing up his things. I need to be back in Regina by the weekend. I have a box of books for you by the back door. Gideon also wanted you to have his camera."

"He did?"

"Mmm. Gideon spoke so highly of you. I believe his exact words were up-and-comer with potential beyond her years. For my brother, that was exquisite praise reserved for very few. This cake is lovely by the way. I never have time to bake any more, but why bother when frozen cakes are so good."

I looked down at my tea and smiled. I wished Elizabeth had been there to hear. When I raised my eyes again, she was holding out a piece of paper.

"This is my address and phone number in Regina. Gideon has left money for you in his will, and I'm to hang onto it until you decide which university you'll be attending. There's enough for tuition and living expenses for as long as you want to go. His lawyer will also be contacting your parents with all the details, but I want you to call me whenever you need help deciding what to study or where to go. I'm an English professor at the University of Regina and know my way around a syllabus."

"But it's too much," I said. "The books are more than enough. My father ... I mean, I wouldn't be able to accept."

"Nonsense. Gideon believed in you, and this is his gift. He never would have left this for you if he didn't want to. My brother was not a frivolous person."

"What if my parents won't let me go?"

"Do you want to study at university, Darlene?"

"Probably more than anything."

"Then I will convince them. I have my brother's resolve once I believe in something or someone, and I will do everything in my power to make his last wish come true."

I nodded. "Thank you."

"You are more than welcome."

"Did Gideon grow up in Regina?"

"No, we grew up in a little town in Saskatchewan called North Battleford. He left after his fiancée married somebody else. He was studying journalism and they were going to get married after he graduated. Not meant to be, I guess."

"It must have been hard on Gideon."

"At the time, it was. Gideon never went back to North Battleford after that, not even for a visit. She broke his heart. I spoke to him every Sunday for the last twenty-five years, and you know, he never once said her name until last week. He never got serious about anyone else either. Some might say he never got over her. He wasn't a man who let on about what was bothering him."

"I didn't even know he was that sick. He told me he had bronchitis."

"He knew last year it was just a matter of months. I spent Christmas with him here. We had a good time and he didn't dwell on dying. He only spoke about his will when he was driving me to the airport."

"It just seems so sudden. Somebody should have been here with him ... at the end."

Phyllis reached across and took my hand. She looked me in the eyes, hers unwavering. "Gideon died the way he wanted to. He had no regrets. I'm glad you've taken in Ruby. She was his only concern, and he'd be pleased she's with you."

"Dad said I can keep her. We've never had a pet before."

"She was Gideon's first dog too. Will you let me speak to your parents about university?"

"Okay. If they let me, I'd really like to go into journalism."

Phyllis laughed. "Somewhere Gideon is looking down on us and saying I told you so. He bet me that you had the itch just like he did at your age."

"I'm going to miss him."

"Me too, Darlene. He was a stubborn old coot, but he was one of the good ones."

The next week crept by. Seven long days of missing Gideon and waiting for summer to end so I could go back to Ottawa. The whole world was coloured grey. Even the weather turned cloudy and cool. I spent a lot of time sitting on my rock watching the waves with Ruby lying next to me. I'd wear my fleece and windbreaker and try to stay warm. Sometimes I wrote in my diary or read books from the Campellford Library.

I avoided Elizabeth except at mealtimes. We'd eat without saying much, then we'd separate: Mom into the store, Elizabeth to the hammock in the backyard, and me to the beach. Elizabeth was very quiet. She didn't insult me at all, and sometimes I caught her watching me when she thought I wasn't looking. I made sure to look away.

I knew that I should be helping Mom in the store, but she didn't ask and I didn't offer. I just felt empty. That weekend, Dad couldn't make it to the lake because he was working overtime in the mill … or at least that's what Mom told me. I wondered if he was finding it as hard to breathe in our house as I was. I couldn't wait for the summer to end so Mom and I could go back to Ottawa.

It was Sunday morning, one that started off cooler than other mornings, but the sun had worked its way out from behind the clouds and burned off the fog. I was sitting on the front steps with Ruby lying next to me on the ground by my feet. Every so often, she'd lift her head and look up the path like she was hoping Gideon would come take her home. I'd reach down and scratch behind her ears, and she'd turn her chocolate brown eyes to look at me. Then she'd let her head drop onto her paws and growl deep in her throat.

"Is Uncle George really going to let you bring that mutt back to Ottawa?" Elizabeth stood at the top of the stairs. I turned to look at her. She was twirling a piece of hair around and around on her finger. She wore a multi-coloured peasant skirt, a green sweater, and her clogs. "I thought animals drove him crazy. Well, maybe crazier."

"He says I can keep her." It was a surprise to me too. "Ruby is my dog now."

Elizabeth clomped down the stairs until she stood next to me. She lowered herself onto the step. "I'm sorry about that old guy."

"Gideon. His name was Gideon and he wasn't that old."

"Well, you know what they say about anyone over thirty. Still, I'm sorry your friend bit it."

"Thanks."

"You must really be in a bad way. You didn't even defend your father when I just called him crazy."

"There's no point. Besides, maybe you're right."

"Yeah." She looked up the road. "I hear a car coming."

I turned to look but couldn't see anything. "You have good hearing. I can't see anything."

"It's boring around here with Danny and Tyler gone."

"Yeah, everyone's leaving." Candy and Michelle had left too, although Elizabeth didn't seem too concerned about them. Of course, they were female. "How long before you go back to Toronto?"

She shrugged. "A week. I'm in no rush. I'll stay till you and your mom leave."

I pretended to grab my heart. "Words I never thought would come out of your mouth."

"What? I've grown to like grooving in nature." She smiled. "Nobody bugging me. Lots of time to read and sleep. I even like looking after kids. They say what's on their mind and don't have any ulterior motives. It's been okay. I've even liked getting to know my little cousin." She poked my in the ribs with her elbow.

"You could have fooled me."

"Which I did. Over and over again."

"You read my diary."

"Sorry. I wouldn't do it now."

We sat quietly for a moment. I thought about how Elizabeth never lied about the big things. She played games, but every so often she let you see something real. I turned and looked up the road.

"You're right. It is a car." I squinted into the sun. "It looks like William's car. He's not supposed to be coming now." I looked back toward the store but couldn't see my mother inside. "Maybe I should just go and see if Mom needs any help."

"I'll wait here and see if it's William," said Elizabeth. She suggestively wriggled her shoulders back and forth. "I'll be his one-woman welcoming committee."

I stood up and smiled down at her. "You really are something else, you know that, Elizabeth?"

She grinned up at me. "So I've been told."

When I saw that it really was William's car, I pushed open the screen door. "Mom," I called. I crossed the floor to the shelves of canned goods. I could hear her moving around in the kitchen. "Did you know William was coming to visit?"

I walked the rest of the way into the kitchen. Mom had her back to me. She was stirring a cup of tea at the counter. She turned and smiled. Traces of watery mascara were on her cheeks. She'd wiped under one eye and the mascara had smeared sideways to her temple.

"Are you okay, Mom? William's coming up the road."

I stood with my arms folded across my stomach.

Mom nodded. She smiled at me. "I'm just being silly. I shouldn't listen to sad songs on the radio." She smiled then stood. She followed me to the screen door then put an arm around my shoulders. We stood without talking and watched Elizabeth run toward the car and open the passenger door. She leaned down and helped somebody out.

"Peg," my mom breathed. She dropped her arm and opened the door. "I never thought she'd come." I followed Mom down the steps and across the grass toward the car.

I wouldn't have recognized my aunt if I'd passed her on the street. She'd put on thirty pounds at least and the long brown hair I remembered was gone. It was now short and permed, with blonde highlights that reflected harshly in the sunlight. I got closer. One side of Aunt Peg's head was more streaked than the other, as if she'd run out of dye halfway through. After we hugged, the smell of mouthwash lingered on my cheek where she'd kissed me.

She stepped back. "My goodness, you're all grown up." She turned and put her arm through Mom's. "Such a long drive. I could use a cup of tea if you're pouring."

I watched them walk up the steps. Aunt Peg stopped at the top and waited for Elizabeth.

"Do you want to go for a walk?" asked William.

I turned toward him and nodded.

We made our way to our stretch of beach and sat in the sand just out of reach of the waves. The sun wasn't as warm as it had been even a week before. We'd be closing up for the season in a few more days.

"What happened to Johnny and Sean?" I asked. "Are they okay?"

"They're safe." William's jaw tightened. He watched the waves for a while. "You judge him, I know, and maybe me." He turned sideways and looked at me. "The way you look at people, Dar. It's disconcerting. Johnny was there, you know. At My Lai."

"When all those women and children …"

"Got slaughtered, yeah."

"Did he … was he in on it?"

"No, but he was one of first on the scene afterwards. That's why he went AWOL. He lost all faith in what was going on. He puked for two days and then took some leave and never went back. Lucky for us, though, he kept a diary and named names. He also got his hands on a report by one of the superiors through a connection he had in the inner circle. It was after the debriefing. So the guy who handed it to Johnny could get court martialled if they find out his name. The air force would like nothing better than to drag Johnny up for court martial and throw him in jail to keep him from talking, report or no. They'd certainly interrogate him too to find out who helped him. We aren't going to let that happen. Now you understand why keeping him safe is so important?"

"Gideon said Candy had some papers she was going to give him. Secret papers. He was supposed to meet her the night of the beach party, but she didn't show up."

"Who knows what she was going to say or do? She was mad as hell at Johnny, well, for a number of reasons." William's voice dropped. "I gave her that ring, the silver ring that Johnny gave to you. He was letting me know that she was done with me." He closed his eyes. His fingers tapped against his cup.

"You can't be sure."

"I'm sure. I knew it was never going anywhere."

"Johnny and Candy weren't … like us. They were like exotic birds or something. Like something we could never have but wanted."

William nodded. "They were just passing through, and we wanted it to last."

"I get it," I said, "but it still hurts when people leave for good. It hurts bad."

William's arm slipped around my waist and I rested my head on his shoulder. "I'm not going anywhere, kid," he said. "You're stuck with me till the bitter end."

"What do you think will happen after the war?"

"I don't think we'll ever go back to what we were. My Lai. Kent State. Johnny and Candy. We might wish they'd never happened, but they did."

"Mom is sad Johnny left."

"I know. This is a time to be sad. But life will get better. We survived Annie's death and we'll survive this summer too, Elizabeth and all."

"Amen to that," I said.

"Amen to that," said William.

Chapter Eighteen

I STOOD IN FRONT of the screen door of our store and looked outside. Elizabeth was sitting on the front steps waiting for her mom and William to go back to Toronto. Her suitcases stood guard near the driveway. She'd lit a cigarette and was waving it around her head to drive away the mosquitoes. I stepped outside and walked down a few steps to sit next to her.

Elizabeth shielded her eyes from the sun and looked up the road. "How many times have we sat here waiting for something to happen?"

"I like it here, I guess," I said.

Elizabeth inhaled then flicked the cigarette onto the step and crushed it with her sandal. She kicked it into grass, then stood and tugged her bell bottoms lower on her hips. They were the same skin- tight jeans she'd been wearing the day she'd arrived.

"Well, the only good thing about my mom showing up is that I get to split from this hellhole early. Thank you, God." She grabbed her hands together and shook them at the sky, then turned and looked down at me. She grinned. "Don't look at me like that. You know I'm just kidding."

"Like always."

"Yeah, like that." She lowered herself next to me and stretched out her legs. "What time are you leaving?" she asked.

"By Friday, if Mom and I get everything put away."

Elizabeth punched my lightly on the arm. "You sure are a hard person to get a rise out of. Usually I get people right where I want them, but you've been a challenge. Just who is the real Darlene Findley anyhow? The girl who tries to please everyone or the girl with the quick comebacks?"

"I could ask the same of you."

Elizabeth laughed. "A couple of words and you've put me in my place. I actually think I'm going to miss you. Who would have thought it?"

"So what are you going to do about Michael when you get home?"

"I'll probably go out with him. Even though I told him to get lost six times this summer, he says he's not going anywhere." She shrugged. "The guy has staying power, I'll give him that."

"What about your mom and dad?"

"They have staying power too, but in their case, it would be better for all concerned if they called it quits and went their separate ways. More humane. You know, they put dogs out of their misery, so why not my parents' marriage? It's not like they even like each other anymore."

"I'm sorry."

"Yeah, well, that's just how it goes. I've learned to live with it, and believe me, I'm going to make damn sure I don't turn out like my mother. Sitting at home with a bottle wondering where my husband is and who he's with. I'm never going to give somebody that kind of power over me. I don't care who he is."

"You don't buy into happily ever after?"

"It's a crock." She glanced at me. "And you?"

I thought it over before answering. "I think it can happen. Not the 'every day is a bed of roses' stuff, but just going in the direction of being happy."

"You sound like a greeting card. Happiness is a direction, not a place. I've outgrown all that crap, and that's the difference between you and me."

William, Mom, and Aunt Peg had finished loading all the luggage into the trunk. Elizabeth was still inside the cottage, another successful avoidance of work. I waited for her near the steps. The screen door creaked open and I looked up at my cousin. She'd put on red lipstick and about six coats of mascara.

"Time to make like a banana and split," she said as she jumped down next to me. "This time tomorrow, I'll be driving up Yonge Street in my new Mustang. If you play your cards right, I'll zip up to Ottawa and take you for a spin."

"I can't wait."

She grinned and reached around my neck and gave

me a quick hug. "Keep the faith," she said into my ear. "God knows, somebody has to."

I watched her walk away, her hips snapping back and forth like a couple of sheets on the clothesline. When she reached her mother at the car, she wrapped her arm around her mother's waist. Aunt Peg reached around Elizabeth's waist and gave her a hug. They stood tight against each other until Elizabeth helped her mom into the front seat. William got into the driver's seat and backed out of the driveway. I was surprised at how sad I was to see them go.

Friday morning. Mom and I had cleaned the entire cottage and store from top to bottom. Dad had just finished calling for the fifth time to see what time we'd be back in Ottawa. We were sitting at the kitchen table having a cup of tea.

"I'm going to have a shower before we get on the road," Mom said. "Did you want to go to the beach one last time? We don't have to leave for another hour."

"Thanks, Mom."

"We'll be back in the rat race soon enough, and you'll be getting ready for school. May as well enjoy today."

I left by the front door and started down the path with Ruby leading the way. When we reached the road, I heard tires slapping on the pavement. The high school kid who'd been delivering the mail since Gideon died was biking toward me. He had the mail bag slung over his back. I was surprised when he stopped alongside and reached into his bag.

"Package for you," he said, thrusting it into my hands.

"Are you sure?" I asked, but he had already started pedalling down the road. "See you next summer!" he called over his shoulder.

I looked down at the flat package. Sure enough, my name and address were on the label. I looked closer and my heart began to beat faster. I tucked the package under my arm and called to Ruby to cross the road. We headed down the path to the beach with Ruby leading the way. We crossed the sand and rocks to climb up to my rock one last time.

I watched the waves for a while. Ruby lay at my feet with her big head on her paws. I thought about Gideon and Annie. I felt like they might be close by, looking down on me, waiting for me to open the package. I turned it over in my hands and took a deep breath before ripping open one end. I slid out one of the magazines. *Country Life*. A white rocking chair on a porch with the lake as blue as sapphire in the distance. Third headline down in dark blue letters: *"Forever Summer at Cedar Lake" by Darlene Findley.*

"Hey, Gideon," I murmured. I flipped to the index, then to page twelve. Below my name was a profile picture of Tyler standing at the edge of the beach and skipping a stone into the lake. My heart jumped again. I began reading. Gideon had tidied up my piece but left all my ideas untouched. It was hard to believe I'd written this. The text wound around a photo of our store taken one bright July day. Time away made it feel like another hand had created this article. But the words were mine.

Every word felt perfect. By the time I finished reading, I knew it was good. I'd captured a place where time stood still while war stole our innocence in Southeast Asia.

The editor had ended with my photo of Candy sitting in the sand, looking out at the water. I'd angled it so that I snapped her back and blonde hair blowing. She looked like she was waiting for something far out past the place where the sky meets the lake.

A few sentences had been added below the text in italics:

Darlene Findley, longtime summer resident of Cedar Lake, future journalist, and light in the darkness. I pass the torch to my talented protegé with pride. Signed Gideon Roberts.

I traced my fingertip across his name. The wind had increased as I sat on my rock reading Gideon's last gift to me. Ruby had shifted positions so that her body rested against my leg. I leaned down to rub her head. Her tail thumped softly on the rock.

After a few minutes of watching the waves hitting the sand and sliding back into the lake, I asked, "You ready to go, then, girl?"

Ruby stood and stretched out her back legs, almost as if she'd understood what I'd said. I let her lead us down the rocks to the beach. I saw Mom standing near the path, looking in my direction with a hand shielding her eyes from the sun. She waved when she knew I'd seen her.

Ruby and I started running toward her.

More Young Adult Fiction from Dundurn

Howl
by Karen Hood-Caddy
978-1926607252
$9.99

Twelve-year-old Robin will never get over her mother's death. Nor will she forgive her father for moving the family to a small town to live with a weird grandmother. At her new school Robin is laughingly called "Green Girl" and is taunted relentlessly because of an award she received. She decides not to care about anyone or anything. But when her pregnant dog plunges into the frozen lake, she saves the dog and hence the puppies.

Robin finds she can't stop herself from caring. She begins rescuing wild animals and rehabilitates them in the barn. Robin's father forbids her to take in more, but she rescues some skunks, anyway, and hides them. Other animals arrive, and soon she's running an illegal animal shelter. When she's found out, Robin mounts a campaign to save her shelter. Will she have the courage to stand against the whole town?

True Colours
by Lucy Lemay Cellucci
978-1926607139
$9.95

Fifteen-year-old Zoe is many things, but confident is not one of them. Perhaps that's why she prefers the company of animals. A self-professed advocate for their rights, Zoe is not above taking matters into her own hands. But the stakes are raised when she finds herself at the centre of a dangerous conspiracy involving the disappearance of animals from a shelter. She turns to street-savvy Alex Fisher, her troubled Social Studies partner, to help unravel the mystery. Zoe soon learns that nothing is as it appears, as she is confronted by angry parents, a dangerous sociopath, and an ill-advised romance.

DUNDURN
www.dundurn.com

Visit us at
Dundurn.com
Definingcanada.ca
@dundurnpress
Facebook.com/dundurnpress

Free, downloadable Teacher Resource Guides

teacher resources
www.dundurn.com/teachers